Idle awhile in Hope County

Fans of Philip Gulley, James Herriot and Garrison Keillor will find themselves at home with Hope County's panoply of humorous, lovable, frustrating, engaging characters.

"You're human," LizBeth *said. "You're allowed to make mistakes." She forced the money into Connie's hands. "Take it."*

"I don't have any way of paying you back," Connie *said.*

"Some day, you'll do for someone else," Lizbeth *said.*

--from "Handout," first place, short story, Westmoreland Arts and Heritage Festival

Praise from fellow authors

"Belinda Anderson creates people who struggle heroically and sometimes humorously with the large and small obstacles of life. In each story, in some way, the characters break through and come out on the other side."

--Meredith Sue Willis, *In the Mountains of America*

"Her short, resonant stories ring in the mind."

--Lee Smith, *The Last Girls, Oral History*

D1082256

Buckle Up, Buttercup

Buckle Up, Buttercup

Belinda Anderson

Mountain State Press
Charleston, W.Va.

International Standard Book Number:
0-941092-53-4
978-0-941092-53-1

Library of Congress Catalog Number:
2008926253

First Edition
Printed in Canada

Cover design by Eric Fritzius (misterherman.com)
Editor: Cat Pleska (catpleska.com)

Mountain State Press
2300 MacCorkle Ave. S.E.
Charleston, WV 25304
www.mountainstatepress.org
Visit the author at
www.BelindaAnderson.com

This is a Mountain State Press book – Charleston, West Virginia. Mountain State Press is solely responsible for editorial decisions.

Dedicated to my sister,
Patricia Ann Jackson

Other books by Belinda Anderson,
published by Mountain State Press

The Well Ain't Dry Yet
The Bingo Cheaters

Contents

Prologue
Twilight Dawn

I may be old and dead, but I am just itching to take a switch to that boy Paul Goshen. Size-wise, I reckon he's a man, but I've never seen a young fellow so bent on foolishness. It's particularly aggravating, because he's got the makings of a good soul. I see him stooping to replace the little flag by his father's grave, just a plot over from my own.

Grandmother says I'm still too attached to Earth, but it comforts me to watch flowers being laid by my tombstone, to know that people still remember this old quilter. I like to spend my afternoons in the celestial garden, resting on a marble bench, poking my cane through the honeysuckle hedge to eyeball the goings on of the living. It's always summer in this garden, with purply butterfly bushes and sugary-smelling pear trees. There's usually several folks here. Most days the children flock around the fountain, where a fat goldfish shoots water out of his grinning mouth. Today the only other spirit here is a man walking by the grape arbor.

Paul straightens and starts to walk away. Then he stops by my grave and I wonder what kind of meanness he's contemplating, but he just bends and yanks the weeds obscuring the "Twilight Dawn Johnson" on my marker.

I've seen him clowning around in class, torturing his teachers. He says he wants to be a police officer, but he'll be lucky if he makes it past his first semester at the community college. And if he does plow through somehow, Heaven help Hope County when Paul Goshen joins the force.

My grave got moved to Hope County to make room for some development project. I was mighty upset at first, but I'm comfortable enough now. Hope County is a West Virginia patchwork of farms, towns and government forest. Big enough to build a hospital and community college, but small enough that people know what time you went to bed and what you bought at Wal-Mart. I made a right smart number of quilts for people in Hope County.

The earth as I see it now reminds me of a quilt, stitched in bold blocks of green, brown, blue and gray. With the mountain ridges crimped just like a pie crust, the world appears to be more the home craft of somebody's great grandmomma than the showpiece of a divine king. The Old Gentleman laughed when I made that observation.

When I say Old Gentleman, I'm not trying to explain the nature of God. The Old Gentleman was how I imagined the Creator when I was a creature of flesh, but this realm is really about spirit. The afterlife is just that — another step along the way to more knowing.

It's a road with potholes. I still don't understand the point of suffering. Can't see how the yoke of slavery did my grandmother any good. Can't see why a good woman like that Edna Simmons, who devotes herself to a feeble mother, can't have a few more dollops of happiness. How come a little girl is left alone on the school bus on a bitter cold winter day? Why does that fellow that's labored all his life have to lose his life's savings? Why can't a vehicle stop in time for a poor dumb animal in the middle of the road?

I keep hankering to get to work straightening out lives, just like I took scraps of fabric from people and gave them back something whole and comforting. But my grandmother says there's more light than I can see making its way to earth and that I got more healing of my own to do.

I know she's talking about Papa. I keep asking to

see him. I can't blame him for asking Grandmother to take me when I was born. How was a poor working man, who had just lost his wife, supposed to care for a baby by himself? But I'd like to know he was sorry to give me up. When I'm ready, I'm told.

So I wait and watch the goings on of the living. Wish I could at least counsel the young women, because I been through my own world of hurt. I reckon LizBeth will eventually figure things out for herself. I especially fret over Dorcas. Much is going to be asked of her and she doesn't yet know she has the strength to deliver. The paths of their lives hold several detours, with that young rascal Paul right at the crossroads.

He appears to be fixing to leave the cemetery, then turns around and flops right down on the ground beside that little flag. "Dad, how am I going to make it without you?"

Next thing I know, the man by the grape arbor is sitting beside me on the bench, his hands on his knees, his back straight as my ironing board, not surprising in a man wearing a dress Air Force uniform. He stares hard through the hole in the honeysuckle.

"That your boy?" I really don't have to ask, not with those matching dimples.

"Yes, ma'am," he says. "He's going through a rough spot."

"He surely likes to spread it around, particularly with his professors." Being dead hasn't cured my blunt tongue.

The officer just smiles. "He's spirited, all right. A lot like I was at that age."

"I thought you military men preached discipline."

"There's a difference between honor and rigidity." The officer looks away from his son to me. "You never knew your own father, did you? You are Miss Johnson, aren't you?" Everybody here seems to know everybody

3

else's business.

"That's me, all right." But I'm not inviting him or anybody else to pick at my stitching. "And who might you be?"

"Ed Goshen."

"Pleased to meet you, Major Goshen." I see that oak leaf on his collar. Maj. Goshen turns back to watch his son, who stands and walks from the graves to a tomato-red pickup truck with fat tires. He jumps in and guns it, spewing dust over all those carefully laid arrangements.

"Sacrilegious," I say.

"Unthinking," Maj. Goshen says. "But he'll learn. He's a diamond in the making." It'd take a powerful squeezing to turn that lump of coal into a gem, but for once I hold my tongue. "Wait and see."

"I might just do that." The soft, pear-scented breeze feels good. "I reckon I've got a little time to spare."

Kicking Against the Pricks

Once I was pretty good at hiding from evangelicals. When I was a kid, they were always trying to trap us in our den. "Drop and roll, kids," Mom would holler and we would flop right off the couch onto the floor and crawl to our bedrooms. Since I had the fastest reflexes, plus being the oldest boy, I was the one that always grabbed the remote and silenced the television so they would think we weren't home.

The Mormons could be tricky to avoid, because they usually sneaked in on bicycles. It was a little easier with the others, because they drove up in cars. I don't mean to sound like a heathen. Mom used to read us Bible stories and we took turns saying grace at meals. So I consider myself a Christian. I checked, just to make sure, in the *American Heritage* dictionary my mom gave me when I enrolled at the community college. That dictionary has really come in handy — it's just the right height to set under my stereo woofer. I found half a dozen definitions and picked the one that suited me, which was "showing a loving concern for others; humane." That was under the heading, "adjective," which I expect to figure out in Developmental English any day now. That's the polite term for the class they make us boneheads take before we can enroll in English 101. I don't know why criminal justice majors have to take English when tickets are the compositions I'll be writing.

The intruders I really dreaded were the ones that wanted to capture us for their congregation. It always irritated Mom, and it irritates me, too, that they assume it's all right to march up to your house and ask you personal questions, like whether you go to church and whether you're even a Christian.

They were after us like vultures. They knew Dad was away, serving overseas, and that Mom had three Sunday school candidates in her house. Mom, who always seemed to be washing dishes, usually raised the alarm from her sentinel post at the kitchen window. At first it was easy to spot them, because they'd get out of their cars toting the Bibles they wanted to quote at us. Then they got sneaky, and the men would hide tracts in their coat pockets. Mom let a couple of those in, thinking they might be from the bank about the mortgage.

Mom set those last men straight. One of them went so far as to say that it was her duty to see that her children were raised in a God-fearing church. "Would you agree that Thomas Jefferson was a great man?" she asked. They allowed that he was. "Thomas Jefferson said he showed his faith in actions, rather than words. He didn't go around telling other people how to run their lives." That got them out the door.

Mom didn't tell me that an evangelical might come disguised as a pretty blonde. I was sitting in the student center, trying to figure out my Developmental English exercises, when she walked in. She looked right at me and came over to my table. I was feeling pretty good about myself and glad I'd worn one of my better caps until she pulled a pamphlet out of her backpack. "Have you been saved?" she asked.

I did it out of pure reflex. I dropped right out of my chair and landed beside an old potato chip. Of course, I realized pretty quick there was no use rolling. I did crawl a little, though, to fetch the snuff can that had spun out of my pocket.

"Are you all right?" the girl asked.

"Oh, yeah." I stood and grabbed my books. "I got to

get to class."

The Developmental English teacher seemed like a nice lady who could use a few iron pills, but I just couldn't get this deal with the parts of speech. I stuck my hand in the air. "Mrs. Travers?"

"Yes, Paul?"

"If an adjective describes a noun, then how come everything that ain't a noun ain't an adjective?" A guy behind me snorted, a girl beside me snickered and Mrs. Travers got this pained look on her face.

"Tell me where you're going with this line of reasoning."

"Take this sentence: The black horse ran rapidly." I had thought this out, and I was ready to rumble. "Horse is the noun. You told us that the noun is what the sentence is about. OK, then, every other word describes the noun."

"But 'ran' is the verb, because it denotes action, and 'rapidly' is the adverb that describes the verb." Mrs. Travers smiled at me.

"No, ma'am, I disagree," I said. " 'Ran rapidly' describes what the horse was doing, so those could be adjectives, too."

"Hey, that's right," the guy behind me said. "That does make sense."

"It's a lot simpler, too," the girl beside me said.

The rest of the group started arguing with Mrs. Travers, and she finally ended the class by asking us to read the chapter again. I felt kind of sorry for her. She had that look that losers get when they don't want to admit the game is over.

I was so pumped that I forgot one of Mom's commandments for avoiding crusaders — stay out of their territory. I was in the student center, rocking the soda machine to get my change, when the blonde walked by. "I see you've recovered," she said.

"Oh, yeah." I scooped up my change. "See you later."

She held out the pamphlet. "You left this before."

Something else Mom taught me was that you had to be firm with these people. "Look, I don't mean to be rude, but I don't care to go around talking religion. I'm like Thomas Jefferson — I'll show my faith in actions, not words."

She slid the pamphlet inside my English book. "I've got to get to class. See you."

I headed straight for the library and went right past the student assistant to the head guy. "You got anything on Thomas Jefferson?"

That same pained look I'd seen on Mrs. Travers passed over him, too, like he wished he hadn't eaten prunes for breakfast. "What is your interest? Architecture? Statesmanship? Horticulture?"

"Religion."

He practically hopped around the reference shelves, pulling out half a dozen books for me. "That should get you started."

I found some great stuff on religious freedom: "It does me no injury for my neighbour to say there are twenty gods, or no god. It neither picks my pocket nor breaks my leg."

In the student center, I found the blonde studying math. I flopped down beside her and got right to the point. " 'Our particular principles of religion are a subject of accountability to God alone. I inquire after no man's, and trouble none with mine.' Thomas Jefferson, 1814."

"Thomas Jefferson owned slaves." The blonde closed her math book. "And DNA tests show that he was the father of the youngest son of one of his slaves."

That washed some of the topsoil off my high moral ground, but I couldn't retreat now. "We're talking about two different things."

"Would you agree that slavery is wrong?" I had a coon dog once with pale blue eyes like hers. I loved that dog.

"Well, sure."

"If Jefferson was wrong about slavery, then he could be wrong about religion, too." She'd pinned me, but good. "What's your name, anyway? I'm Dorcas."

"I'm Paul."

She laughed. "Figures. Paul kicking against the pricks."

"*Excuse* me?"

"You know, the road to Damascus. When a light shone on Saul and a voice said to him, 'I am Jesus whom thou persecutest: it is hard for thee to kick against the pricks.' "

"So you're talking about a guy named Saul, not Paul."

She pushed that long blonde hair back. "At the time, he was Saul and he persecuted Christians. After he heard the voice, he was blind for three days. Then he was miraculously healed and as Paul became a great preacher." She smiled at me. "Why don't you come to our Easter sunrise service? It's outdoors, and you can just walk away if you don't like what you hear."

She really did have pretty eyes. "Outdoors where?"

"The Old Stone Cemetery."

"You're having services in a graveyard?" That was just weird.

"It's symbolic of Jesus rising from the dead."

"Gotcha." I pushed my chair back. "I appreciate the invitation." No way was I going to get up before dawn and stand around freezing in a graveyard.

Then she touched my hand and I was as whipped as Mrs. Travers with the adjectives. "I'll look for you,"

Dorcas said. She opened her math book again and I walked away.

I might go to that sunrise service if I don't have anything better to do. But there's no way I'm going to Sunday school.

She can take the kids if she wants to, though.

Bark Like You Mean Business

The village lay under two feet of snow, with drifts at the windy corners. In a sky of iron the points of the Dipper hung like icicles and Orion flashed his cold fires.

Mariah Travers drove along the interstate, trying to concentrate on the audio book she had borrowed from the library, hoping to distract herself from the anxiety of entering her community college classroom.

She'd started the semester with high aspirations, for herself and her students. Developmental English could be so much more than remedial punishment. It could launch a love of language, of the way words dance together like atoms bonding to form matter. But so many of her students seemed only to want just enough English instruction to pass, to move quickly toward the associate degree that would land them better jobs.

Mrs. Travers — she had to insist on being referred to by a title of respect — flipped her windshield visor against the glare of the harsh afternoon September sun. Her car was sealed against the late summer heat, the air conditioning providing a whispering background whir to the words of Edith Wharton. *The night was perfectly still, and the air so dry and pure that it gave little sensation of cold.*

Her Great Aunt Lenore had once waded through three-foot snowdrifts to fetch a doctor for her mother. At midnight. With only a sliver of moonlight to guide her steps, the vicious wind having blown out her lantern. Or so she said. Hard to tell the difference sometimes between fantasy and reality.

Exiting the interstate, Mrs. Travers paused just long enough at the stop sign to be polite and had just pulled out into traffic when her car expired. Hearing the squeal of brakes and the blast of a horn, she looked in the rear-view mirror to see a mini-van swerving, just missing her vehicle.

Mrs. Travers possessed a number of talents, several related to grammar, but quick reflexes were not among them. The type of teacher who never entered a classroom without a lesson plan in hand, she was abysmal at dealing with troublesome students, like that smart-aleck Goshen boy.

A nightmare carousel of color and sound surrounded Mrs. Travers as vehicles whipped around her, honking and flashing their lights. She had just located the emergency flashers when a Jaguar pulled over in front of her. It might have been green in color – difficult to say, covered as it was in a coating of road salt. She wondered from where he possibly could have been traveling, but the powder obscured his license plate.

As the driver approached her car, she lowered the window, losing the last of her air-conditioned ambiance. "Do you have a cell phone? Could you call for help?"

The older man, dressed in black pants, tooled boots, snowy shirt and bolo tie, stood comfortably, his brown, lined face suggesting many hours in the sun. He looked as though he were dressed to call a square dance. "I'm not much for gadgets. I could offer you a ride, though."

As Mrs. Travers considered how she could gracefully decline an invitation into a stranger's car, a tow truck lurched onto the shoulder. "Thank you, sir, but I'll be fine."

"You sure about that?" He seemed very kindly, but he was a stranger.

"I'm sure."

As he departed, a young man walked up. "Looks

like you could use some help."

"Please," she said to this Boy Scout, this gallant knight clad in a gray work shirt with an embroidered patch that read *Skunk*. She tugged at her own pale blue blouse, making sure it was tucked properly in her skirt.

"I can tow you to my dad's garage." Skunk spit. Another snuff dipper, just like that noxious Goshen boy. He quoted a figure.

"That's fine." It actually seemed exorbitant, but Mrs. Travers desperately wanted to exit the shooting gallery. Skunk continued to stand in silence before she comprehended the meaning of his hesitation. "You need payment now." She found her checkbook and handed over the fee.

Skunk scrutinized the check. "How long you had this account, Mrs. Mariah Travers? You got any identification?"

She fumbled to find her driver's license. "I just moved here. I teach English at the community college." She did not feel compelled to enlighten him that technically she was no longer Mrs. Travers, or that she was here to make a fresh start in this mountain valley called Hope County.

"I hated school," Skunk said. "I like to read, though. You ever use Stephen King in your classes?"

"Um, no," Mrs. Travers said, keenly aware of the hiss of air brakes as a tractor trailer hurtled down the exit ramp.

Skunk was undisturbed. "See, that's why I always hated school. Stephen King kicks that Hawthorne guy's ass."

Mrs. Travers's eyes were fixed on the rear-view mirror as she waited to be punted into the next county. But the trailer eased by, and she stepped out of the car and into instant humidity. Immediately, she started sweating, and she knew it was just a matter of time before her hose melted right onto her flesh. "Can you drop me off at the college?"

"I could, but it'll cost you extra."

"What?" Mrs. Travers began to feel uneasy about this transaction.

"Helps us cover the liability insurance."

She handed over another check and climbed into the truck, without any assistance from Skunk. As Mrs. Travers buckled the grimy seat belt, she noticed a cheap graphic novel on the seat. "Oh, you like Edgar Allen Poe?" She tried not to inhale too deeply of the rancid pine essence radiating from a cardboard cutout dangling from the rear-view mirror.

"Yeah, I picked that up at the dollar store. He's pretty good."

"I bet you'd like Jack London. Have you ever read *Call of the Wild*?"

"Some kind of hunting story?"

"In a way; there's a hunt for gold. And a kidnapping. And fights." And lessons about loyalty and self-reliance, but she decided not to press further. "I'm sure you could find it at the library."

"Right," Skunk said in a way that persuaded Mrs. Travers that he would not be delving further into classic literature.

It was going to be one of those afternoons. One student had brought her 10-month-old baby because her cousin, who was her babysitter, had a hair extension crisis. Mrs. Travers wanted to protest, but as the student pointed out, what could she do? The baby spit out its pacifier to drool and smile winningly.

Mrs. Travers tried to collect the homework she'd assigned, but only half of the class seemed able to locate the necessary paperwork. Anxiety began gnawing at Mrs. Travers, but she gamely tried to project her voice above the din of conversation, attempting to begin a discussion of the parts of speech.

Paul Goshen raised a hand. "If an adjective describes a noun, then how come everything that ain't a noun ain't an adjective?"

Mrs. Travers despaired, but she ignored the snorts and snickers and invited Paul to explain the reasoning behind his question.

"Take this sentence: The black horse ran rapidly. Horse is the noun," he said. "OK, then, every other word describes the noun."

Mrs. Travers smiled with relief. This she could remedy easily. "But 'ran' is the verb, because it denotes action, and 'rapidly' is the adverb that describes the verb.' "

The scholar disagreed. " 'Ran rapidly' describes what the horse was doing, so those could be adjectives, too."

"That does make sense," another student said. One after another began chiming in agreement.

Mrs. Travers attempted to battle with the students, who had become more animated than she'd ever seen them. The baby chewed contentedly on his mother's grammar text, finding solace for his teething troubles. Finally, Mrs. Travers admitted defeat and simply asked the class to read the chapter again.

She strode down the hall to the faculty lounge, hoping to consult Julia Donovan, but found no one there. She had to tip the coffee urn to procure half a cup of stale liquid. Maybe she should start bringing a Thermos, filled with something stronger than coffee.

Mrs. Travers carried the foam cup to her office, where she called the garage. Based upon a repair her ex-husband had once made on his car, she had a strong intuition that the problem was her alternator, a situation easily remedied.

Nope, the alternator was fine, said the male voice on the line, a voice that sounded older than Skunk. The car stopped because the timing belt broke.

Mrs. Travers brightened. A belt would be even cheaper, and probably quicker, to replace. "So I can pick it up?" Surely someone at the college could give her a ride.

The man laughed and anxiety stirred anew within Mrs. Travers. "Not hardly. You've got an interference fit engine. When that belt broke, the pistons shot right into the valves."

"That sounds serious."

"Oh, yeah." He quoted her a repair price that would have made her stagger had she been standing, but what could she do? She'd just have to wait a few more weeks to get her hair cut. Maybe she could delay the mammogram that would have to be paid from her insurance policy deductible.

"So when will my car be ready?"

"It'll take about three days."

Three days without a car, in a rural county with no cab service. She didn't know her colleagues very well, but maybe she could persuade one of them to give her a ride. Preferably *not* Julia Donovan, whose eyesight was notoriously unreliable. "So I can pick up my car Friday afternoon?" She felt the need to be specific.

"Sure."

Using her tongue to pry her clenched teeth apart, Mrs. Travers said, "I'm fine," in response to Julia Donovan's offer to wait just to be sure everything was in order. Mrs. Travers's colleague had very nearly T-boned a turning driver's ed car, in addition to absently running a red light while discussing the miserable state of post-modern literature. Mrs. Travers firmly shut the door on the carnival ride and strode into the brown block building proclaiming itself as Seward's Service Center.

Inside, she found a vestibule, adorned with three split black vinyl chairs. A woman who looked far too ancient to be driving was seated upon one of them. She reminded Mrs. Travers a bit of her Aunt Lenore in her stout physique. But Aunt Lenore's hair had been the color of old tin, while this elder wore a crown of snowy white. And while Aunt Lenore favored metal as an adornment, this woman was draped in a massive turquoise necklace. Her tanned, wrinkled face and rough hands led Mrs. Travers to deduce she'd labored long years outside, perhaps tending to crops.

Magazines, mostly of the hunting and fishing variety, littered a cheap coffee table. Mrs. Travers couldn't believe the cash register had been left unattended.

The ancient one paused in her perusal of an old science magazine. "There's an article here says you can bend spoons and change time on a clock, just with your mind." When Mrs. Travers responded only with a smile, the woman asked, "You looking for Old Man Seward?" Mrs. Travers supposed she was. "Through there."

Mrs. Travers opened the door and walked into a cavernous, oily-smelling service bay. A man who surely must be Skunk's father and another man, a huskier version of Skunk, appeared to be enjoying some version of high tea, swigging sodas and gobbling take-out chicken wings that smelled even stronger than the aroma of engine oil. Skunk sat in a corner on an overturned crate, reading a lurid comic of *The Black Cat*.

"Excuse me," Mrs. Travers said, addressing her remarks to the older fellow. In appearance, with his bushy gray eyebrows and the red shop rag draped from his back pocket like a flag, he reminded her of the genial mechanic

17

who used to tend her parents' vehicles, always producing a mint or stick of teaberry gum for her. "Is my car ready?"

The old man paused in his chewing. "Part didn't come in." The image of the genial mechanic faded.

"Which part?"

"If I told you, you wouldn't know any more than you do now."

Mrs. Travers knew her Aunt Lenore would never have tolerated such disrespect. It was said that she had once pounced upon a man who neglected to remove his hat in church. Her earrings, necklace and brooch jangling like an armed Crusader, she grabbed him by an ear and hauled him outside as though he were a juvenile truant. But what could Mrs. Travers do? She didn't want to anger the men who would be patching her means of transportation. "So when will my car be ready?"

"Monday." He pulled out the red rag, wiped his hands and stuck it back in his pocket. "Tuesday for sure."

She called Monday. No part. She called Tuesday. The part had arrived, but had not been installed. "Can't get anything done for answering the phone," Old Man Seward said, as though the situation were Mrs. Travers's fault.

Wednesday, she learned the repair had been made, but in doing so, Skunk had discovered the exhaust manifold was cracked.

"How much will that cost?" She gulped at the price, but what could she do?

Friday, she was told that while Skunk was underneath her car, he'd noticed one of her wheels was cracked. It seemed an incredible coincidence. "Now look here," Mrs. Travers began, determined to stop an escalation she could not afford.

"If you're not picky, we could try to scrounge up a used one from a wreck at the junkyard."

Mrs. Travers did not want to ride on a wheel from a

wrecked car. Diverted from her righteous protest, she said, "No, no, that's fine."

She hung up the phone, wondering how in the world she could pay this mounting bill, which would exceed her credit card limit. She contemplated calling her ex to borrow the money, but could not bring herself to dial the number. She didn't want to admit her attempt at independence had already proved a failure, and she dreaded the inevitable lecture. *Don't put up with that nonsense. Tell them you want your car, and you want it now. Tell them you'll call the attorney general's office. Tell them you'll call the Federal Trade Commission.*

Mrs. Travers went home to her apartment, ignoring the boxes still waiting to be unpacked. It seemed pointless to set out a tea service when microwaving a mug of hot water would suffice for one person. Instead, she picked up Jack London's *A Daughter of the Snows*, seeking an escape from her own world by entering another.

The ice was picking up in momentum, and the hum growing louder and more threatening. It had been a long day, and Mrs. Travers began to drowse, lapsing into a luscious nap filled with satisfying images of the garage goons laboring beneath piles and piles of icy snow, thrashing with their wrenches to escape an avalanche threatening to engulf them.

She awoke heartened, and decided she wanted a cup of Earl Grey, brewed properly. Rising and opening one of the cardboard boxes, she carefully extracted several wads of newspaper, opening one to reveal a pot, the next a lid, and finally cups and saucers. She smiled, remembering the tea parties she'd had with Aunt Lenore, who'd been surprisingly gracious in serving young Mariah's favorite doll and teddy bear.

Aunt Lenore had given her niece the set as a wedding gift, along with unsolicited advice: "Remember, sometimes you have to stand on your hind legs and bark like you mean business." But Mrs. Travers could never bring herself to bark.

In her married life, Mrs. Travers had only brought the set out at Christmas, because the pot's decoration featured a Victorian ice-skating party. She absently contemplated the scarf-wrapped men and fur-muffed women on the pond, remembering one particular summer tea party with her aunt. Mrs. Travers had just completed first grade and with her vast education had become skeptical of Aunt Lenore's stories.

"I remember the year it snowed on the Fourth of July," Aunt Lenore began.

"It can't snow in July." A hot breeze swept through the screen door.

"You don't think so?" Aunt Lenore closed her eyes, breathing deeply for what seemed a long, long time. She opened her eyes, took her niece's hand and led the little girl to the doorway, pointing to the fine white particles floating in the air. When Mrs. Travers tried to tell her parents of the miracle, they laughed and said she must have seen bits of cottonwood fluff tossed by the wind.

Mrs. Travers still wasn't so sure that her aunt hadn't been able to change the weather through force of will. She turned her attention to the ritual of making tea, pouring hot tap water into the pot to warm it. As she concentrated on her task, she found herself making decisions. She'd call Monday morning and say she was picking up her car. If she held off on that last repair, she could just squeeze the charge through on her credit card. Cracked wasn't the same as broken.

"It's your funeral," Old Man Seward said the next morning when Mrs. Travers called, having just finished a cup of strong English Breakfast tea.

"What — what do you mean?" she asked, her

resolution beginning to dissolve.

"Wouldn't drive it in that condition myself."

Mrs. Travers wavered, but holding one of her aunt's cups gave her courage. "I'm picking it up."

"Suit yourself." Old Man Seward said and hung up.

Mrs. Travers obsessed about her car throughout the day, paying little attention to the background class conversations that usually compelled her to attempt to exert discipline. Julia Donovan's driving managed to get her attention, however, and when they arrived at the garage, Mrs. Travers found her hand cramped from gripping the armrest.

"I'd better wait this time."

"No, really I'm fine." Mrs. Travers walked into what would have been the customer reception area in any other establishment. The only sign of life was the white-haired woman, who looked as though she hadn't moved. In fact, Mrs. Travers was fairly certain she saw a spider web stretching from one ankle to the tiled floor.

"Look here," the old woman said, holding up a magazine with a picture of a half-naked monk. "Some fellows from Harvard tried to freeze him. They stuck him in a 40-degree room and wrapped him in cold wet sheets. And do you know what happened?"

"What?" Mrs. Travers asked, her mind on her car, but wanting to be polite.

"Steam started coming off those sheets. He was drying those sheets with his body heat. Just sitting there, meditating."

"How interesting," Mrs. Travers said. "Excuse me," and she walked on to the door to the service area.

Inside the thieves' den, she found the father and the husky son snacking on pork sausage biscuits. Skunk sat comfortably ensconced in his reading nook, biscuit in one hand, a comic version of *White Fang* in the other.

"Hope you brought a tow rope," Old Man Seward said.

"And why is that?" Mrs. Travers asked, the familiar tincture of anxiety already beginning to creep back into her heart.

"Clutch is gone."

Mrs. Travers was not a mechanical genius, and not the best judge of human nature, considering her marriage, but this sounded even lamer than the flimsiest of her students' homework excuses. Anger swelled within her.

Threaten to call the attorney general's office, she could hear her ex-husband advising.

Instead, she closed her eyes, hoping to calm herself. She knew she did not have the confidence of Aunt Lenore to win a verbal confrontation.

But her mind declined to give her calm. Her imagination churned, wishing oblivion upon these tormenters.

A yelp caught her attention and she opened her eyes. On this hot September day, snow was falling at the entrance of the service bay. Fast, fat flakes began piling at the open doorway. Wind swept through the service bay, swirling the precipitation into a blinding storm.

Skunk dropped his comic. "It's snowing," he announced.

"Score one for the boy genius," his brother said. "Help me close this door."

But the tracks were already frozen. The door refused to budge.

"It can't be snowing." Skunk shook his head, sending bits of white flying.

Beyond the bay door, Mrs. Travers saw a UPS truck pull into the parking lot of the nearby Dairy Queen. The driver, never glancing back at the snow globe scene, jumped out of the truck, wearing shorts, and hurried toward the restaurant with what he seemed to think was a heavy box. She saw her would-be Samaritan from the interstate, exiting with an ice cream cone, pause to hold open the door.

Shivering, Mrs. Travers picked her way in her heels through the accumulating snow to her car, pleased to find the keys already in the ignition. As she slid in, the old man, his brows crested with snow, hollered at her, "Hey, you haven't paid."

"Oh, yes I have," Mrs. Travers said. "I've paid dearly." *Bark like you mean business.*

She shut the door and started the car. Her left foot engaged the clutch and she shifted smoothly into reverse, driving through the couple of inches of powder already accumulated. Clearing the bay, she paused to note that her tracks already had disappeared. The snow fell even faster and thicker. The brothers tried to sweep it away with shop brooms, but the blizzard lapped around the ankles, then their calves. One last look found the men lurching around in snow up to their knees.

Mariah Travers turned her attention forward and drove into the sunshine.

Mr. Kotes

I knew it was going to be a long semester my first day in English 242 when the professor proclaimed her passion for British authors. All I wanted to do was fill another requirement on my way to an associate degree in criminal justice.

But Dame Julian seemed determined to make us love Jane Austen and all her lawn bowling buddies. To the Dame's face, we called her Professor Donovan. Her first name was Julia, and one of the students at the community college came up with Dame Julian after actually reading the assignment on the mystic writings of Julian of Norwich.

The Dame wasn't as intimidating as her nickname implied. She reminded me more of a fairy godmother, tiny and with silvery hair and green eyes. If she could, she'd produce a wand and whisk us all to an enchanted England, where ladies with umbrellas and men with pocket watches drank afternoon tea.

"My dear Mr. Bennet, have you heard that Netherfield Park is let at last?" It was going to be a really long semester. No wonder Lewis Carroll hurled Alice down a rabbit hole. I'd be nutty as a hatter myself if I had to hang out with this bunch. "And so the plot begins to unfold." Dame Julian stopped and squinted toward the door. It was the first cold day of the season, and we'd piled our jackets in one of the chairs. Dame Julian addressed herself to the lump of fabric: "I'm sorry, I can't seem to place you—"

"Coats," spoke up Joe, the theater major always quick to spot the potential for fun.

She picked up a slim blue record book from her desk. "How do you spell that?"

"K-o-t-e-s."

"Mr. Kotes." She held the book to her nose. "I don't seem to have you on my roll."

"Add/drop," Joe said, adding a little tobacco country flavor to his tone, but wisely choosing to play the interrogated witness and offer no more than he was asked.

"I'm glad you decided to join us," Dame Julian said. "Now, let us return to Miss Austen." And that's how we found out that Dame Julian was as near-sighted as a mole.

Joe dutifully began answering the roll for Coats. It was the perfect joke — Dame Julian lectured nonstop, never pausing to ask questions or invite them. But I almost blew the gag the day I topped the pile with my baseball cap. Dame Julian squinted in that direction, then asked, with some hesitation, "Mr. Kotes, are you wearing a hat? Hats are not permitted in the classroom." The pile just sat there. "Well, Mr. Kotes?"

I got out of my seat and grabbed the cap. "Didn't you hear the lady, dude?"

"Take your seat, Mr. Goshen," she told me. Then she started droning on about Charles Dickens. Somewhere between *The Pickwick Papers* and *A Tale of Two Cities*, I got my idea. Dame Julian didn't assign papers, probably because she couldn't see well enough to read them. Our grades would be based solely on the mid-term and final exam. We figured she probably made her husband, a biology professor, read them aloud to her.

No homework meant no need to actually show up for class. We'd leave a few warm bodies for show, but Joe could answer the roll for most of us. We could read the assignments at our leisure, then doubletalk our way through the mid-term, which no doubt would be an essay exam. I began sketching a rotation schedule in my notebook, and Dame Julian beamed at me for writing so industriously.

I presented my game plan during lunch at the student center. Everybody thought it was a great idea, except Joe. "I can't do female voices," he said.

"If he won't do them for us, it wouldn't be fair to do them for you guys," said Brandi, a blonde that I would have paid more attention to if I weren't hooked up with Dorcas. And if she didn't have the irritating habit of peeling the labels off her beverage container. At the moment, she was deconstructing the wrapping around a bottle of apple juice.

"Where would Jack Lemmon and Tony Curtis be if they hadn't played women?" I asked. Personally, I didn't see what was so funny about two actors in drag trying to hide in an all-female orchestra, but Mom always cackled every time she watched that old movie.

"Jack Lemmon's dead." Joe got up from the table and went over to a vending machine.

"What about Pyramus and Thisby?" Brandi asked, scraping another bit of paper from her bottle and adding the piece to her pile of confetti.

"Who?" Joe scooped a candy bar out of the chute.

"You know, Shakespeare, *A Midsummer Night's Dream*," Brandi said. "If you're going to be an actor, you might have to play Thisby."

"Forget it," Joe said.

I reconsidered. "There's another option," I said. "Ladies and gentlemen, let me show you the drop-and-roll method." My mother had taught me as a child how to slide off the living room couch and crawl to the bedroom at the first sign of an evangelical type in our driveway. "After you tell the Dame you're present, here's what you do." I demonstrated the move, dropping to the floor and creeping silently along until I came to a pair of shoes and jeans.

I looked up at my beloved, Dorcas. "Do you have epilepsy or something?" she asked. That was how we'd met, me dropping and rolling out of reflex when she tried to give me one of her church pamphlets. Luckily for me, today she was in a hurry. "I can't have lunch with you, Paul. I've got a new work-study job." She stepped over me and marched on.

The system worked perfectly. I had worked out the rotation schedule to leave no noticeable gaps. After roll call, students would begin slithering out of the room, one by one, until about a fourth of the room had emptied. I was feeling pretty proud of myself until Dorcas found out. "You ought to be ashamed of yourself," she said.

"It's the Dame's own fault," I said. "If she'd get glasses or contact lenses, she'd know what was going on."

"She can't wear corrective lenses," Dorcas said. "They give her headaches." As a work-study student for the English department, Dorcas now was an expert on the faculty.

"Not my problem." I got up and left before she could hypnotize me with those pretty blue eyes into doing something foolish, like attending all my classes.

Joe came close to blowing the whole deal. It was a day when I was cursing my luck at my turn at the rotation. Dame Julian was expounding upon how *Bleak House* was the best novel ever written by Charles Dickens. It was worse than spending all morning in a deer stand, where at least a fellow had some hope of action.

Joe couldn't take it. I was looking around the classroom, desperately trying to find something of interest, maybe a fly trying to winter inside, when I noticed his head dropping to his chest. He began to snore, softly at first, then with more enthusiasm.

Maybe she couldn't see, but Dame Julian could hear just fine. She stopped, gaping in astonishment that someone could fall asleep during her discussion of characterization. Stepping forward and walking tentatively down the rows, Dame Julian peered at each of us. No one could nudge Joe, who was surrounded by empty chairs. She got right in my face, and I could see the anger and confusion in hers.

She began working her way down the next row, headed straight for Coats. If she began poking Coats, we were all as good as dead. Suspended, for sure. Joe continued to nap in bliss, a thin line of drool starting to snake down his chin. Dame Julian advanced down the row and I saw my dreams of wearing a uniform evaporate. Then fortune caused Joe to choke and he woke with a snort.

Dame Julian's head whipped around. Nothing but silence. She stood there, uncertain, then walked back to the front of the classroom and resumed her lecture, a sorrowful expression on her face.

After the scare passed, I was sure we were invincible. I was in a pretty good mood during the mid-term, making up stuff and throwing in a "therefore" here and "consequently" there. I went on Thanksgiving break so primed that I bagged a six-point buck the first day of hunting season. I kept the head in a locker cooler in the back of my pickup so I could show my buddies.

Then my luck ran out. After returning to school from break, I made my way to English class, ready to collect my mid-term result. I knew I'd passed. Might have even finessed my way to a "B." I was the last one to show up and she asked me to hand out the papers before I sat down. I couldn't help but notice a trend as I passed out paper after paper, one failing grade after another. Finally, I sat down, stunned by my own scarlet letter.

Dame Julian called the roll. When she came to Coats, Joe answered as usual. The Dame paused. "Mr. Kotes, you don't seem yourself today." She strode forward, no hesitation in her step, her hefty copy of *Vanity Fair* in hand, until she stood before our pile of winter wear. She gave Coats a good whack with Thackeray, sending jackets and scarves flying to the floor. She returned to the front of the room, picked up a stack of papers and began handing them out. It was a list of homework and paper assignments, enough to keep me out of the woods for the rest of hunting season.

Brandi protested immediately. "You've got a ten-page paper with six sources due next week."

"That's correct." This was no fairy godmother standing before us, but a silver-haired avenger blazing green fire from her eyes.

"And there's another one due the week after."

"Also correct."

Joe spoke up. "You can't do this. None of this stuff is on the original syllabus." Joe, who knew exactly how many absences were allowed before automatic expulsion, considered himself an expert on institutional policy.

Dame Julian's new glare fastened on him. "If you'll refer to that document, you'll discover a line that says the syllabus is subject to change." She opened her book. "I suggest you take notes. There may be a quiz Friday."

Ninety minutes later, I slunk out of the class, seeking comfort from Dorcas. I found her in the cafeteria, eating an apple and actually studying.

"Laser surgery," Dorcas said. "Slices the cornea. She had it done over break."

"And you didn't see fit to tell me about this development?"

"*Whatsoever a man soweth, that shall he also reap.*" I was trying to come up with that line about cleaving unto your man when she fixed me with those sky-pale eyes and patted my hand. "Better to learn now that actions have consequences." She absently rubbed my hand and I found myself thinking a lot about sowing and reaping.

The class sweated those first couple of weeks under the regime of the new, improved Dame Julian. I nearly wept over my assignment to analyze humor and realism in the English novel. But I didn't think she could maintain the pressure — she just didn't have the personality for revenge. And Dorcas said she'd overhead the Dame telling another teacher that she was starting to see halos around lights. I figured the Dame would soon tire of reading our papers.

On one unusually warm Friday, Dame Julian stood for several minutes looking out the windows. *"What fine weather this is!"* She kept standing there, while I worried that she'd designed some new torture for the class. "Class dismissed," she finally said. "Never mind the reading assignment on the revised syllabus. Monday is going to be show-and-tell. Bring in something beautiful, with a relevant quote from a British author."

"What do you mean, something beautiful?" asked Brandi. "Like jewelry?"

"Something from the natural world would be more appropriate."

"That's it?" asked Joe, suspicious of this change in the Dame.

"That's it," she said, and turned back to her window gazing.

I figured I could find something in the woods to bring back to Dame Julian. Maybe a crow's feather or a creek rock. And maybe I'd collect a squirrel or two for myself.

Monday morning, I returned to English class with a box for Dame Julian. I hadn't shot any squirrels, but I'd found a special treat for the professor. Some small part of me, a chunk of conscience that Dorcas had been trying to nurture, scolded me, telling me not to be such a jerk. But I knew the Dame's reaction and the laughs I'd get from my classmates would be worth any fallout. I set the box and the quote on her desk, along with all the other treasures the other students had brought.

Dame Julian walked into the classroom and

switched off the overhead lights. "I think it's bright enough without these," she said. She stepped over to her desk and clasped her hands. "People," she said, "This is just marvelous." She picked up a rock, perfectly round. *"The stone often recoils on the head of the thrower.* I don't recognize that quote."

"Queen Elizabeth," piped up Joe. "She said it to Mary Queen of Scots before she had her whacked."

"I'm not sure a monarch qualifies—"

"She's British," Joe insisted.

"I'll give you credit for ingenuity," Dame Julian said. Next, she picked up a nest. *"The swallow leaves her nest, the soul my weary breast,"* she read. "Ah, Thomas Lovell Beddoes, nineteenth century poet. Excellent."

Next came my box. She glanced at the paper underneath. *"A wise old owl lived in an oak; the more he saw the less he spoke."* Dame Julian shook her head. "Is this someone's idea of a joke?"

"Check the reference," I called out.

She did, then smiled. "Edward Hersey Richards, another nineteenth century poet. Very well, Mr. Goshen." Still smiling, she opened the box. The smile congealed, then slid away. Watching confusion and disgust crossing her face wasn't nearly as entertaining as I had imagined. The final expression, one of hurt, made my gut ache. "Do you care to offer an explanation?"

"It's an owl pellet," was my feeble reply. I heard Joe snort.

Moments crawled by while she looked steadily at me until self-control returned to her face. I was pretty sure those were tears making her blink. "My husband tells me these are remarkable archives. *Nature is a self-made machine, more perfectly automated than any automated machine.* Eric Hoffer. He was American, but it's an apt quote, don't you think?" She plucked the pellet from the box and broke apart the gray mass. I never dreamed this tea-party type would even touch such a thing. "All this fur leads me to guess the day's prey was a mouse." Carefully, she withdrew an entire miniature skeleton. "*Rigid, the skeleton of habit alone upholds the human frame.* Virginia Woolf."

Some of the girls, and a couple of the guys, looked ill. After all, the Dame was playing with an owl's hairball. "*Sight is the least sensual of all the senses,*" she said, more to herself than the class. "*We strain ourselves to see, see, see — everything, everything through the eyes, in one mode of objective curiosity.* Yes, indeed, Mr. Lawrence." I didn't know who she was talking to — there wasn't any Lawrence in the class.

"This is what the owl was unable to digest. But note that it wasn't afraid to take in whatever it could find to sustain itself." Dame Julian cradled the bones and fur in her palms. "The wise owl swallows life in big gulps, then expels what it cannot use."

I waited for her reprimand, and knew I deserved whatever was coming. Instead, Dame Julian fondled the delicate skeleton for a few moments, then walked over to me.

"This is too fine a gift, Mr. Goshen." She held out the pellet remains, and I couldn't think of anything to do but to take the mess from her. "Keep this. And remember."

Her hands closed over my cupped ones, and she gently but firmly squeezed. Her small hands forced mine shut, and I felt the pressure crushing the small skeleton. "Remember."

Fruit of the Spirit

A man will do a lot of things for love, but I never figured I'd be delivering fruit baskets to the elderly just because of a blue-eyed blonde.

"Remember, Paul," Dorcas said as she drove up to Widow Persinger's sagging A-frame, "to say the Community Church congregation wishes you the blessings of the season."

"Maybe you ought to give the speech. I'll just hand her the basket." I yearned to help myself to that succulent Red Delicious, lying so temptingly in the basket at my feet. Ever since I was little and Mom had milk and a peanut butter sandwich waiting for me after school, I've always hankered for an afternoon snack.

Dorcas gently slid the transmission into park, as smoothly as she does everything. She's the one who packs fruit for charity, gets involved in student government, works part time and maintains a scholarship, while I find myself pulling last-minute all-nighters to pass basic community college entrance courses. "No, I have to extend the invitation to Sunday morning services."

When I got out, that shiny apple rolled onto the floorboard and I stuffed it in my jacket pocket. I follow the two-second rule for food retrieval — it can't collect germs if you pick it up immediately.

I picked my way around some patches of ice, following Dorcas up the steps of the porch, which appeared to have been attached to the house as an afterthought by a crew of drunken monkeys. Gray clouds drooped in the sky, threatening to dump more trouble.

Widow Persinger opened the door before we'd even

had a chance to knock. She presented the impression of a dandelion nearly gone to seed, with a head of wild silvery hair stuck on a skinny stem of a body. "Merry Christmas," Dorcas said, looking like one of the heavenly host in her powder blue parka.

"Here you go," I said, shoving the fruit basket at the old woman. Dorcas glared at me and I added, "The Community Church—"

"A fruit basket?" Widow Persinger held the gift as if I'd handed her a pail of rat poison. Of all the looks I expected to pass across the recipient's face — gratitude, joy — anger was not the emotion I would have banked on. "A fruit basket? How dare you!"

Dorcas, confused, tried to continue with our shtick. "We would like to extend—"

"Fruit baskets are for the old and sick." Widow Persinger appeared to be working herself into a state of outrage. "Or the needy," she added, with disgust. "Do I look old or sick or needy?"

As a criminal justice major, I could quickly evaluate the evidence. But before I could speak, Dorcas said in that soothing voice that makes me volunteer to change the oil in her car, "No, of course not, it's just—"

"Then get the hell off my porch and leave me alone."

"The time is come for thee to reap; for the harvest of the earth is ripe," Dorcas said. "Revelation 14:15." Seemed to me that was a reference to the apocalypse, but I kept my mouth shut and started backing up.

"I will also reject thee, that thou shalt be no priest to me," shot back the widow. "Hosea 4:6." I had begun easing my way down the steps when she winged me with a banana. "And take your rotten fruit with you!"

I accelerated my retreat, with Dorcas right behind me, a tangerine whizzing by her ear as we touched ground and started to run for the car. Then, ignoring a shower of pecans, Dorcas stopped. "The land shall yield her fruit, and ye shall eat your fill," she called. "Leviticus 25:19."

"Though ye offer me burnt offerings and your meat offerings, I will not accept them," hollered the widow. "Amos 5:22."

A ballistic grapefruit sent us dodging behind the one shelter in the yard, an old maple tree. "Now what?" I asked. "We'll never make it to the car."

"What do you mean now what? You're the criminal justice major."

"Oh, I can tell you what the textbook advises. Call for backup." The tree blocked a hit from a pear, a ripe one by the sound.

"To handle one elderly woman?"

"Especially in the case of an elderly woman." I reached in my pocket for the apple. I needed fortification for the siege.

"Did you take that apple from that poor woman's basket?" I thought I detected a touch of wrath in her voice. "Don't you dare eat that apple. That's supposed to go to someone elderly or sick or—"

"Needy," I said, about to take a bite. Then, with my acute law enforcement intuition, I realized the barrage had ceased. "She's out of ammo. Let's go."

"We can't just leave her like this. We're here to witness, remember?"

"I've witnessed plenty for one day."

"She's just a scared old lady." Dorcas stepped out from the safety of the tree. The scared old lady shot a juicy kiwi that splattered the front of that pretty parka.

I waited for the ground to begin trembling from the righteous indignation of Dorcas. She is a certified nut when it comes to neatness and appearance, maybe because her family's never had very much. Dorcas even irons her jeans.

At least that's what her mother told me she was doing the last time I sat for fifteen minutes waiting for her. "That stain will never come out," she said in a low, low voice. I saw anger filling her face. "It took me six months to get this coat out of layaway."

Dorcas took a step forward. "Now, you listen here—"

"What, no Bible quote?" The widow grinned with muscles that hadn't been used for awhile. "Not feeling so high and mighty now, are you? Chew on this: 'But the fruit of the Spirit is love, joy, peace, longsuffering, gentleness, goodness, faith. Galatians 5:22.' " The widow's grin grew bigger. She reached into what should have been an empty basket and drew forth an orange.

Sometimes, a man has to take charge. I darted around the tree and fired the apple, aiming to knock the orange out of her hand. Instead, I scored a head shot, and the widow toppled.

"You've killed her!" Dorcas cried, racing up the steps to the porch.

"It was just an apple, and besides—"

"Help me get her out of this cold."

Inside, we found plenty of Christmas cheer, if fruit baskets count. One, emitting the odor of produce past its prime, sagged on the coffee table. Another, still sealed in cellophane with a tag from the Presbyterians, sat on the floor of the living room, beside a puffing humidifier. All the old ladies I knew filled their shelves and walls with pictures of children and grandchildren, but the only sign of family in this house sat on the television, a framed picture of a young man in a uniform standing beside an Esso pump. We dragged Widow Persinger to her plastic-protected sofa, where she began to whimper.

"Find a phone and call a rescue squad," Dorcas instructed me.

The widow rose like Lazarus, probably an old classmate of hers, and grabbed Dorcas's arm. "The only way anybody is hauling me off is when I'm dead."

"But you might—"

"Just go in the kitchen and get me a cup of coffee," the widow ordered. "Did you wipe your feet?"

Dorcas gave me a look and I scooted to the kitchen, where my nose detected the smell of overripe fruit faster than my eyes could take in the grove of gift baskets cluttering the counters and table. Fruit flies sailed around the conglomeration, not seeming to care what denomination they sampled.

I opened a cabinet, found a mug smothered in a pansy print and poured a cup from the coffee maker. As I passed the kitchen sink, I heard the dripping of a leaky faucet. "You got any tools?" I asked the widow as I handed her the coffee. She was sitting up now. "I could probably fix that leak if I had the right wrench."

"Which leak?" the widow asked, then shook her head, an action she seemed to immediately regret. "Doesn't matter. I don't have any wrenches." Having her skull rattled seemed to have taken some of the fight out of her.

"I've got a toolbox in the trunk of my car," Dorcas said. Of course she did. Not only did she have an Allen wrench set, she had a cam tool and I tightened the adjusting ring to stop the sobbing spout.

"All done," I said, reappearing in the living room and ready to depart.

"You don't reckon you could have a look at the toilet, do you?" the widow asked, sweet as a fig now, sipping her coffee. "That toilet's been running, and I know it's wasting water."

Luckily, all I had to do was bend the float arm and adjust the water level in the toilet tank. When I returned to the living room, I found Dorcas with screwdriver in hand, adjusting the pneumatic closer on the widow's storm door and telling the widow she'd be back with a recipe for pear butter. By the time it was dark, we'd cleaned the furnace filter and cleared the gutters just as the sky began dumping snow on us.

Widow Persinger could not bring herself to actually thank us, but she did send us off with, "On the good ground are they, which in an honest and good heart, having heard the word, keep it, and bring forth fruit with patience. Luke 8:15."

Dorcas zipped her parka tight as we left the house. "I think we both learned something valuable today."

Walking behind her, I spied the Red Delicious, now a dark lump on the porch, and scooped it up, wiping it on my sleeve and taking a big bite.

"Didn't we?" Dorcas asked.

My teeth sank again into that crisp flesh, just as juicy and sweet as the day it departed the tree. "You bet," I said.

Blue Cadillac

Boyd heard the rolling rumble of the garage door and rushed outside, cursing. She'd done it again.

He planted himself at the side of the driveway, between the dogwood trees flowering in the triumphant resurrection of spring. He didn't dare try to actually block his wife's exit — Goldie never used the rear-view mirror — so he stood between the bushes, waving and shouting.

Slowly, slowly the '59 Cadillac backed out and stopped. The electric window on the driver's side dropped a few inches. "What?" Goldie asked. She looked good behind the wheel of a luxury sedan. Not many women her age could or would wear their hair long, and she'd chosen to remain a burnished blonde, too. She wore a knit pant suit of ocean blue, nearly the same color as the car.

"How about a lift?" He'd decided to try the light touch. He gave her the grin that had charmed her when they first met on a seniors bus tour to the musical mecca of Branson. Boyd's good looks had given him the edge over that possum-faced Jack, even if he did own a fuel oil distributorship. Boyd was still a golden boy, though his tan was turning leathery and his thinning hair, like Goldie's, required chemical assistance. He, in turn, was attracted by Goldie's classiness. She didn't chatter nonstop like the rest of the women on the trip. She could sum up just about anything she had to say in one sentence.

"You know I can't do that." He heard her shift from park to reverse.

"Why not?" It was the same question he asked her every Sunday afternoon.

"Because Daddy wouldn't like it." The car began to

creep backward.

Boyd laid his hand on the hood, still cool from its nap in the garage, and she stopped again. "Your daddy won't know anything about it." Goldie's ancient father, a GM dealer, had died three months ago, leaving the Cadillac, a houseful of antique furniture and a sizable settlement to Goldie, with very specific instructions that the estate would go to cousins — not Boyd — upon Goldie's death.

Goldie maintained the Caddy as a moveable shrine. Once a month, the guy in the Suds on the Run van arrived to shampoo, shine and buff the car. And every Sunday afternoon, Goldie took it out for a few hours, to keep the oil stirred, she said. But she never invited Boyd. She tried to make it up to him by bringing him a Wendy's Frosty, double bagged to protect the car's interior, saying, "Something sweet for my Sweetie," but she'd started sneaking out when the chocolate confection failed to mollify him. Now she tilted her round sunglasses, big as black moons, toward the sky. "It would be disrespectful."

"Just how do you figure that?" Boyd knew he was inviting trouble, but he couldn't stop himself.

"Because Daddy never liked you." And with that, the window whined shut and the car accelerated backwards.

Yanking his hand from the hood, Boyd stepped back, brushing against the lilac. The intense sweetness offended him, and he slapped at the irritating branch. He watched Goldie cut the steering wheel sharply when the suspension dipped at the curb. As the front tires hit the street, she straightened the wheel and drove forward, never once having turned her head.

It was true, the old man had hated him, called him a "Goldie Digger," just because he was ten years younger than Goldie and had moved into her house when they got married. And now this.

The worst part of it was that Goldie didn't even appreciate what she was driving. The 1959 Cadillac Fleetwood Series Sixty Special Sedan was top of the line, looking ready to rocket with those gigantic fins and snappy bullet tail lights. He'd tried to get Goldie to sell the car just to spite her father, but what Boyd really wanted was to slide behind the wheel of the blue beauty.

Boyd was not going to let that old goat get the better of him, even in death. The following Sunday, he praised Goldie's lunch of roasted chicken, then sat and watched her clear the table and run the water in the sink for the dishes. Offering to help never occurred to him. She was so particular that she wouldn't hear of a housekeeper, though she could easily afford it.

A top-of-the-line dishwasher sat unused in the kitchen; instead, she handled the Fostoria glasses and Fiesta Ware plates as though her mother's spirit inhabited them. If he broke one of those heirlooms, he'd never get inside the car.

The plan was so simple he couldn't understand why he hadn't thought of it before. He would simply shadow her and hop in the car as soon as she unlocked it. If he could only get inside, a turn at the wheel would come next. It irked him that she locked the Caddy, even in the garage, but he wouldn't mention it today. He sat at the kitchen table and watched his wife plunge her hands again and again into the soapy water. This was taking forever. His prostate gland started to agitate and he got up and headed for the bathroom. Maybe she'd have progressed from the plates to the pans by the time he got back.

But when he returned, the kitchen was empty. Boyd rushed out the front door, just in time to see Goldie backing out of the garage. She hesitated when she saw his wild waving, and he seized the opportunity to sidle around to the passenger door. Before he could lift the handle, he heard the unmistakable snick of the electric door locks.

This was too much. He marched around to the driver's side. The electric window lowered an inch. "Boyd, we've been through all this before. You know I can't take you with me."

"Why do you have to drive it at all?" Maybe whining would work.

"Daddy wanted me to take care of it, or he wouldn't have left it to me." He couldn't see the expression behind her dark sunglasses, which made strategy difficult.

"Where do you go, anyway?"

"Wendy's, of course."

"Besides there."

"Nowhere special." And then she was gone, the chrome of the Caddy twinkling in the sun.

Nowhere special. It had never occurred to Boyd that the destination might be the real reason Goldie didn't want him tagging along. She was meeting somebody. That weasel Jack, who'd been divorced four times, twice more than Boyd.

Boyd's imagination gnawed on that scenario for days. He envisioned Jack's ropy arms wrapping around Goldie's soft shoulders and he nearly confronted her, but instead decided to bide his time. Sunday, as soon as Goldie began clearing the table, Boyd announced that he needed a nap.

He did go into the bedroom. He'd been watching Goldie closely all week, and now he knew where to find those car keys. Lifting the lid of a mahogany jewelry box, Boyd grabbed the Cadillac medallion key ring. He sneaked into the garage, unlocked the doors, then silently returned to the bedroom to deposit the key ring back in its nest.

The sound of water running in the kitchen assured him he still had plenty of time. He carefully made his way back into the garage. He opened the driver's side door and a back passenger door. Next, he clicked the lock on the driver's door, closed it and climbed in the back seat, shutting that door behind him. He stretched out on the passenger bench, congratulating himself on his cleverness. Goldie never checked the mirrors. She would never know he was back there. And he was going to find out just what the hell was going on.

He heard the door to the garage open, then caught the faint gardenia scent of Goldie as she got in and started the car. Ever so slowly, the Cadillac crawled in reverse, hesitated at the curb, then gently began to accelerate forward. Goldie turned on the radio and began humming along to some oldies station. The Cadillac streamed ahead, the gentle highway vibrations lulling Boyd into sleep.

When he awoke, the Caddy was parked. Cautiously, he raised his head just enough to peek out a window. Surely she wasn't meeting Jack at the Piggly Wiggly. Just then, Goldie emerged from the grocery store, carrying half a dozen yellow roses wrapped in tissue paper.

Boyd dropped back onto his berth and stewed. He'd never heard of a woman buying roses for a man. Why was she buying flowers for that dried-up prune? How come she'd never bought flowers for him? He was as sensitive as the next fellow.

Goldie started the car, but she didn't turn the radio on again. She drove and drove, with Boyd growing madder by the mile. He didn't deserve this kind of humiliation. He was a good husband. Didn't he give her back rubs without her even asking? And it was always up to him to remind Goldie on Thursday mornings that she needed to set the garbage out.

The Caddy began slowing down. Boyd heard the tires crunching on gravel. Aha. She was meeting Jack at some out-of-the-way spot. Boyd couldn't wait to see their faces when they realized he'd found out their dirty little secret. He might even punch Jack in the face.

The car climbed a knoll and stopped. When Goldie got out, the smell of fresh-mown grass and a cool breeze drifted into the car. He almost leapt after her, then figured he'd better make sure Jack had arrived. Boyd raised his head and saw a tableau of tombstones spread over a hillside. His wife was meeting her boyfriend in a cemetery.

He rested his chin on the sill and watched her walking away with the roses. Gradually, he realized that he'd been to this place before, when Goldie's father had been buried. And then Boyd began to sweat with shame. His wife was sneaking, all right, but not to meet Jack — she thought she had to steal away to grieve for her father.

Goldie knelt at a mammoth granite headstone. She removed a wilted bunch of flowers from the monument's stone urn, unwrapped the grocery store roses and arranged them in the vase. She had to grab the tombstone to haul herself to her feet, and she stood there a long time, gripping the carved stone. Just as she turned, Boyd slid back into his prone position.

Boyd lay in misery on the drive home, remembering how many sour remarks he'd made about her father. The car slowed and turned, and then he started at the sound of a speaker squawking through Goldie's lowered window. She was ordering his Frosty. Uh oh. His plan hadn't taken into account the drive-through. As Goldie rolled up to the window, Boyd closed his eyes and hoped the cashier would think he was napping and wouldn't say anything.

No such luck. Boyd heard the clink of change, then a young female voice saying, "I see you're carrying cargo today."

"Hmm?" Goldie's voice hesitated. "Yes, I guess so." And then the Caddy was moving again.

Boyd released a breath he hadn't realized he was holding. Whenever Goldie wasn't sure of the direction of a conversation, she would agree with the speaker rather than risk asking a question that might reveal ignorance.

He rehearsed a dozen resolutions during the trip home. He would never speak another ill word about Goldie's father. He'd help clear the table. He'd bag the trash and put it in the can to save her time on garbage mornings.

The Caddy slowed and turned and rolled into the garage. Goldie slid out of the car, clicked the electric locks and lowered the garage door. Boyd heard the door to the house open and shut before he understood that he was trapped. He hadn't considered this, either, during the formulation of his plan.

Debating with himself whether he was limber enough to crawl over the seats, he heard the door to the house open again. The electric locks clicked and suddenly he felt the cool air of the garage wreathing his head. Boyd gaped upside down into the face of his wife.

"You want your Frosty, or not?" she asked.

He was caught, run to ground. He'd just have to talk his way out of it. He sat up. "Goldie, hon, I'm sorry, I never realized, I never understood before—"

"I know." She didn't seem angry.

Encouraged, Boyd got of the car. "Now I get the picture. Look, I don't mind going to the cemetery with you. We can go together next Sunday." Maybe she'd let him drive now that they'd cleared the air.

"No," Goldie said.

"No?" So she was mad at him, after all.

Goldie patted his arm. "Don't worry, I'll still bring your Frosty."

Boyd tried to sort through his confusion. "I don't care about the Frosty," he whined. "Why can't I go?"

"Because," Goldie said, giving him a gentle smile. "Daddy never did like you."

Buckle Up, Buttercup

LizBeth was shaking the grit of Route 60 from her sandals when the police car roared by, then stopped and backed up. Great. Just her luck.

"Trouble, ma'am?" The cop that emerged from the cruiser was her age, and possibly cute. Hard to tell with that dopey hat and uniform, but the dimples compensated. The badge on his chest identified him as P. Goshen.

Sunburned and dusty, wearing a ridiculous pink gingham dress with puffy sleeves, LizBeth stood on the gravel shoulder of a secondary road surrounded by fields of corn and maple-covered mountains. An old lady in a Cadillac convertible had nearly mown her down, and some jerk had tried to lure her into his truck. She'd sent him on his way by yanking a nail file from a pocket in her dress and plunging it in a tire. "Looks like you've got a slow leak," she had advised him. "Better get to town before you go completely flat."

"No, sir," LizBeth now said politely. "No trouble at all." They were too young to be calling each other "sir," and "ma'am," but he'd started it.

"This road isn't particularly accommodating of pedestrian traffic," Officer Goshen said. "Maybe I could give you a lift into town."

LizBeth was not in the mood to answer questions. "I'm fine."

"I'm afraid riding is your only option." He was a good six inches taller than LizBeth. She liked that. "Seems the Beckley police are looking for someone that matches you pretty well." Officer Goshen politely opened the front passenger door. For a few seconds, she considered running.

But the only sanctuary in sight was a muddy pond, fully occupied with grumpy cows twitching in irritation at flies. She got in the car.

"Buckle up, Buttercup." Officer Goshen removed his hat.

"Excuse me?" LizBeth turned her best glare on him and was gratified to see his face redden.

"I'm sorry, that's what my mom always told us kids. I didn't mean anything by it." He paused. "But you do have to fasten your seat belt."

LizBeth buckled up and the car moved forward. "Just tell me one thing. Is he still alive?"

"Oh, yeah," Officer Goshen said. "And mad as hell."

"Shouldn't I be sitting in the back seat, wearing handcuffs?"

"I got the cuffs, but I'm not exactly sure what I did with the keys," Officer Goshen said. "And something tells me you're not a career criminal."

"Don't let the dress fool you. I'm more dangerous than I look." She wanted to see if P. Goshen could smile.

"Oh, you look plenty dangerous, all right." He produced a smile, with dimples, that made her glad she'd shaken out the stupid braids she had to wear at the restaurant. "Mind if I leave the windows down?"

"Suit yourself."

Just as he crested a hill, the old blue Caddy popped into view, well over the yellow line. P. Goshen dropped two wheels off the pavement, veered around the massive missile and calmly steered back onto the road.

"Aren't you going to stop her?"

"What for?"

"I don't know, maybe reckless endangerment or something."

"Nah, it's not like she cracked some redneck over

the head with a pepper mill."

LizBeth could feel her cheeks heating beneath her sunburn. "Believe me, he asked for it." LizBeth did not appreciate strangers touching her personal self, and particularly not in especially personal places.

"So why run?"

"I thought I'd killed him." She could still remember her surprise at how he'd dropped to the floor, unconscious, blood pouring from his head. While the manager called for an ambulance and everyone else crowded around the victim, LizBeth, dazed, had simply walked out of the restaurant and kept walking right onto the interstate interchange. That was the story of her life, react first and regret later. Like quitting school and running away from home just on the notion that she could go to Nashville and sing.

A pepper mill, even a big heavy wooden one, was pitiful protection against psychopaths and crazed drug addicts, warned the female trucker who had picked her up and lectured about the dangers of the road for the forty miles to the next truck stop. That was when LizBeth looked down at her lap to see she was still carrying the weapon. At the truck stop, LizBeth threw the pepper mill in the trash, and resumed walking. She bypassed the interstate ramp, figuring she'd better stick to the side roads. She had no idea where she was going, but she knew from movies that fugitives had to keep running.

LizBeth looked over at P. Goshen. "It took me several miles to figure you probably couldn't kill someone with a pepper mill."

"But you kept on going."

"I wasn't sure what kind of reception might be waiting on me back home." LizBeth ran a hand through her dark hair and knew P. Goshen was looking at her sideways.

"If anyone will not welcome you or listen to your

words, shake the dust off your feet when you leave."

"Excuse me?"

P. Goshen blushed. "I go to Bible study with my girlfriend."

"Sounds serious." Whoever she was, LizBeth knew she wasn't right for P. Goshen. He needed a woman who didn't mind a holster hanging from the bedpost.

"I reckon so."

LizBeth adjusted the neckline of her gingham getup. It wouldn't hurt for him to notice what he was missing.

Instead, he seemed intent on another approaching vehicle. This time, he turned on the strobe and pursued the car a good mile before it finally pulled into a parking lot.

"Excuse me," he said. "Back in a minute."

Though the driver remained in the car, LizBeth thought she discerned the silver hair of a senior citizen. The exhange she could hear through the open windows confirmed her conclusion.

"I noticed you're not wearing your seat belt."

"I always wear my seat belt."

"You're not wearing it now."

"I must have unbuckled it when I pulled over."

"No, ma'am, I observed you driving without it."

"I've been driving since before you could wipe your own backside, and I always wear my seat belt. Always. And I don't know how you could see anything besides that girl. What are you doing with a girl in your car?"

"She's a person of interest."

"I'll just bet she is." LizBeth heard the engine of the other car starting again. "See, I'm fastening my seat belt. You better hope Dorcas doesn't see you with that person of interest." She drove off.

Dorcas. So that was the name of the girlfriend.

"Do you ever give anybody a ticket?" LizBeth asked when Officer Goshen returned to the patrol car.

"Oh, sure," he said, but she had her doubts. They drove to an old two-story brick building and parked. LizBeth looked around for the police station. "Upstairs," he said. He got out and opened the car door for her. A real gentleman. They entered the town hall and walked past the assessor's office. The fossil at the desk whistled and laughed. "Paul's gone and arrested Heidi." Paul. His name was Paul. LizBeth had always imagined she'd end up with a Steve, but she could work with Paul. Or maybe she'd just call him P. Goshen.

The police station turned out to be three small rooms. The very-pregnant secretary handed P. Goshen two messages. "Hey, Celeste," he said. "Where's the chief?"

"He's meeting with the mayor."

P. Goshen looked at the messages and turned to LizBeth. "Seems your customer's wanted in another state on a drug warrant."

"Do I get a reward?"

"Don't push your luck," P. Goshen said, but he smiled. He looked at the other message, then frowned. "Excuse me a minute." He went to a desk in a corner and parked himself at the telephone.

The secretary, her round stomach pushed back from her desk, stared at LizBeth. LizBeth stared right back. "Want the name of my designer?"

"You've got a bug in your hair." Celeste turned her attention to a computer screen.

LizBeth had just removed a disgusting little worm from her hair when a blue-eyed blonde walked in. Had to be the girlfriend. LizBeth eyed the competition. Pretty, sure. But she looked like she might be bossy. "You poor thing," the blonde said to LizBeth. "What happened?"

LizBeth was considering any number of snappy comebacks when P. Goshen walked over. "Battery."

"Oh, how terrible for you," the blonde said. "Listen,

I'm a social worker, let me—"

P. Goshen interrupted. "She's the perpetrator."

"Oh," the blonde said, and backed up a step. "I just stopped by to make sure you got my message that we'll have to meet the floral designer a half-hour earlier."

"Just picked it up. Sorry, Dorcas, but no can do."

"You mean you can't leave earlier?"

"I mean I can't leave at all." P. Goshen twitched a thumb in LizBeth's direction. "Got paperwork to process."

"This is the third time I've rescheduled."

LizBeth, uninvited, sat in a chair beside the secretary to watch the proceedings. Fluid pulsed where her toes had chafed against her sandals, the pressure building to form painful blisters. Gently, she spread her gingham skirt over her sunburned legs and plucked at her pink puffy sleeves, actions that seemed to irritate Dorcas, who said, "Can't this wait?"

"Crime never sleeps," P. Goshen said, with what LizBeth considered saintly patience. "Is it really a big deal? We'll just make another appointment."

The assessor wandered in. "I need my stapler back." Celeste, mesmerized, did not look away from the couple, but groped on her desk for the stapler and handed it to the assessor.

"No, it's no big deal." The blonde's blue eyes froze into icy chips. "It's just our wedding. Just the biggest day of our lives."

"But, hon, it's still six months away."

The assessor, making his way to the door, stopped. "Six months? You should have made your arrangements a year ago." He winked at LizBeth.

The blonde folded her arms across her chest. "Try telling that to him."

"Dorcas, we're just talking about flowers." LizBeth detected weariness in P. Goshen's voice. She suspected

Dorcas could nag a man into a coma.

"Just flowers." LizBeth expected Dorcas to grow hysterical. Instead, the fiancée's voice dropped to a low, calm tone. She slowly withdrew a modest diamond ring from her finger and deposited it on the frog-eyed secretary's desk. "Better to learn now than to regret later." She turned to the assessor. "Proverbs 29:11." And with that, she was gone.

LizBeth waited for P. Goshen to rush after Dorcas, to sweet talk her into taking his ring back. Instead, he returned to the corner desk and dropped his head in his hands. LizBeth and Celeste stared at each other until the latter finally said, "There's a big Bible in the courtroom." The secretary hustled out and returned with a ragged book bound in black leather, flipping through the pages of the Old Testament. "Here we go: *A fool uttereth all his mind: but a wise man keepeth it in till afterwards.*"

They resumed staring at each other until LizBeth got up and went over to P. Goshen. "I can stay here with Celeste until you get back. I swear on my discarded pepper mill that I won't try to escape."

P. Goshen lifted his head. "She's right. Better to break it off now than to regret it later."

He looked so vulnerable, so cute, but LizBeth said, "She's what my folks call a good woman."

"She's a hell of a woman," P. Goshen said.

"She's worth going after."

"I can't make her happy," P. Goshen said.

"Probably not," LizBeth agreed, her impulsive tongue asserting itself again.

P. Goshen yanked his head upright. "Let's talk about your situation."

"Can't you just let me go, since the guy's a criminal, anyway?"

"Entirely separate incidents."

LizBeth picked at a puffy sleeve, pulling it back from her reddened flesh. She was going to peel, for sure. "What happens if I'm convicted?"

"It's a felony," P. Goshen said. "You could serve a year."

A year of her life for acting without thinking.

"What does being a felon mean?"

"For starters, you can't vote until you complete your sentence. Oh, yeah, and you'll be prohibited from ever using a pepper mill again." P. Goshen paused, but LizBeth didn't smile. "You know, possession of a deadly weapon."

LizBeth didn't answer. Pageant contestant versions of herself paraded in her mind. Gliding first across the stage came the deluded girl dressed in a cheap sequined outfit that failed to impress Nashville. Next marched the gingham lass, displaying her talent for convincing herself she was not stuck in a dead-end job. Finally, the inmate shuffled into the spotlight, wearing a boxy and bright orange jumpsuit.

P. Goshen was talking again. "Did the guy actually accost you?"

"He grabbed my—" LizBeth began, but P. Goshen kept talking.

"So you were in fear of your safety?"

"Well, I don't know that I was—"

She was interrupted by Celeste, who had walked over to butt in. "You *were* in fear of your safety, *weren't* you?"

"Yes," LizBeth said, catching on. "I was in fear of my safety."

"Sounds like self defense to me," P. Goshen said. "Let me call the guys in Beckley."

Five minutes later, LizBeth was a free woman. "The Beckley police aren't interested in charging you," he told her. "Seems you're more trouble than you're worth." He smiled, but it wasn't the carefree grin she'd seen before. Dorcas had left with a chunk of his heart.

"I don't have to go to prison?"

"Not unless you want to take a tour of the facility."

LizBeth stood and headed for the door.

"Where are you going?" P. Goshen asked.

"It's a long way to Beckley," LizBeth said, trying to ignore her aching feet. "Might as well get started."

"I'll take you home," he said.

The idea of inviting Officer Goshen inside her apartment was an appealing one, especially if she pushed away the image of two days' worth of dirty dishes piled in the kitchen sink and the laundry flung across the sofa. But she walked down the stairs and out of the building without speaking. Dorcas might not be the right woman for him, but she wasn't, either. P. Goshen followed, then strode on to his patrol car and opened the passenger door.

Her feet betrayed her, leading her body to seat itself in the sedan. P. Goshen slid behind the wheel. "I'm more trouble than I'm worth."

"I figured that out already," P. Goshen said. "But I'm a professional at handling trouble." He smiled, with his dimples, and this time the shadow of Dorcas was diminished, replaced by real warmth. He started to pull out from the parking space into traffic.

"Hey, wait," she said.

"What now?"

"Buckle up, Buttercup," LizBeth warned. "This could be a bumpy ride."

Sanctuary

Dorcas sought the sanctuary of the forest, craving comfort for her wounded heart. Here, cradled by the evidence of creation, surely she could find some peace. But the natural world cared nothing for her broken engagement. Crows laughed and gossiped in the high branches of the hemlocks shading the walking trail. Though autumn had arrived, withering the leaves to pale yellows and crumbling browns, the weather remained hot and sticky. Gnats swarmed around her sweating and teary face as she hiked up the steep incline.

She heard the sound of footsteps stirring the fallen leaves before the man appeared around a curve. And then, blocking the trail, stood her former betrothed, a shotgun slung against a shoulder, a dead squirrel dangling by the tail from his free hand.

Having altered her daily routine to avoid intersecting with him, she stood and stared at the countenance she once thought she'd see every day for the rest of her life. She used to worry about how that nose would look on their children, but had always figured the dimples would compensate. It hurt her to see the hunter's victory grin fade as he recognized her, to know that her presence could extinguish the light in someone's face.

"This is awkward," she finally said.

"For you and me, maybe," Paul said. "I don't reckon he much cares." Paul indicated the squirrel with a jiggle, causing the corpse to sprinkle droplets of blood. "You doing all right?"

Dorcas tried not to stare at the grotesque remains of the squirrel's head. She'd never been hunting, never seen the slaughter required to produce chicken tenders and hamburgers. "Are you really going to eat that?"

"As my truck is my witness." Paul repositioned his shotgun. "I'll get Mom to fix me some biscuits and gravy to go with it."

A gnat decided to dive beneath her eyelashes just as she was about to succumb to the tempting notion of suggesting that Paul ask the alluring LizBeth to prepare his kill. Reaching to pluck the mote from her eye, she rediscovered her wet face.

"You all right?" Paul repeated.

"I just came out here to think." Once again, Paul shifted his gun, and she knew he would rather be anywhere than in the presence of a crying female. "I'll be fine."

"Look," Paul said. "I never meant for things to turn out like this."

"Everything happens for a reason," Dorcas said. "This must be God's will."

"I reckon." Paul began to edge past her on the narrow trail. "I got to get going if I'm going to make my shift. You ever need anything, you call me. I mean it." And then he disappeared around another curve in the trail.

She knew he meant it. She knew he had a good heart, and she had loved him for it. Dorcas yearned to call after him right then, to say that what she needed was him. If she spoke right now, they might have another chance.

Instead, she turned and began walking again up the trail, wondering whether pride or prudence had muted her. The humid air pressed against her as she struggled uphill, swatting gnats and stumbling on tree roots. Dorcas stopped at the top of a ridge, breathing hard in the thick, wet air. She made her way to a fallen log, sat and closed her eyes, hoping the slight breeze would dry the perspiration sliding down her forehead and mingling with her tears.

Her closed eyes lulled her into a meditative state,

and she found herself praying for deliverance from her heart's pain. She sent her prayer, as always, to an image of an enthroned figure shrouded in blinding light, too glorious to behold.

I am not who you imagine. Dorcas's eyes popped open at these words that had come unbidden to her brain. Direct communication from God was reserved for long-dead mystics. No doubt she was just all wrought up, as her Aunt Lee would say. She closed her eyes again, willing her mind to become quiet.

I am not what you imagine. She jumped up from the log and began walking rapidly again. This whispering in her mind could not be a divine communication. The only people God spoke to in modern times lived in mental institutions. Dorcas tried to summon her picture of a supreme being safely removed at a distance, but her comfortable image of a king on a crystal throne had shattered.

I dwell here. The soothing cadence of the whisper began to calm her. Instead of attempting escape, Dorcas now found herself stopping and surveying the majestic landscape before her, the blue hills covered with the green of spruce and pine, a few specks of gold and red already showing on the maples. *I dwell here.* Her ringless left hand, she saw, now lay over her heart. How could divinity dwell in something that was broken?

From pain rises love. This not-voice must be debris from her subconscious, leftover snippets from the self-help gurus blaring from the televisions of her clients' homes as she tried to teach them what came naturally to dumb animals, the caring of their offspring.

How could love rise from pain? From the evidence she'd seen, the victims of pain most often turned it on others. The victims of war, once liberated, grabbed any chance to become the oppressors. Once, she'd arrived at a client's home to find a boy crying at being robbed of a plastic action figure by his older brother, then grabbing a toy from his small sister and grinning as she shrieked in indignation.

Dorcas had thought she and Paul would have children right away. She'd even been entertaining thoughts of becoming a full-time mother and homemaker if he could earn a promotion. As a caseworker for social services, she wasn't making the difference she'd hoped. So many of her clients simply gave lip service to the service plan that was supposed to transform their lives, offering just enough compliance to qualify for assistance. Struggling to cope with the chaos she saw every day, she longed for an orderly little nest of her own, with a sweet-cheeked baby and a loving husband.

The chime of the cell phone in her jeans pocket roused her. It seemed obscene to use a phone in this silent haven, but she was on call at the department, and it could be an emergency.

It was. The department had been summoned by a police officer answering a neighbor's report of abuse and neglect. Dorcas recognized the names and address immediately. She hurried to her car, where she grabbed a lukewarm bottle of water. Gulping half of it, she started her car and began driving to the Hope County Housing Project. The first time she'd been called there, she'd met Brittany and Kevin, transplants from Virginia, and before that, Maryland, and prior to that, Florida.

The door to the second-story apartment stood open, showing Dorcas a repeat of her first visit: dirty clothes strewn carelessly, the smell of urine and rotting food, the roar of a television, the sight of Brittany and Kevin sprawled high or drunk on the sofa. The only difference was that Brittany had gained weight, and in the place of a toddler sucking soda out of a bottle was a filthy pre-schooler with matted hair, sitting on the floor and playing with a fire truck missing a wheel.

Dorcas pressed her lips tight together, trying to suppress her anger. She'd gotten Simon removed to foster care, but a talented attorney had persuaded the family court judge that Brittany and Kevin had repented and wanted nothing more than to have their own son back. What they wanted, Dorcas had been sure, was the continuation of benefits to support their habits.

Paul, dressed in his uniform, came walking out of the bedroom, carrying a bundle. Dorcas swallowed her unease at running into him again. They could behave like professionals.

"Unbelievable," Paul said. He handed the bundle, a wadded up blanket, to her. Some sort of evidence, she supposed, reaching to grab it. "Careful," he said. "Contents fragile."

And then she saw that he was handing her a baby, or the specter of what should have been a baby.

"I've called the rescue squad," Paul said. "I'm guessing this little girl needs an IV, fast."

Dorcas trembled with pity at the sight of the pathetic little pinched face. Gently, she folded back the blanket to find match-thin limbs and a bloated belly. The slight shift caused a twitch of pain in the baby's face. Without opening her eyes, she mewed, too weak to cry in protest. *From pain rises love.* What good could come from the suffering of this innocent spirit? Trying to keep her voice low, to avoid disturbing the baby further, Dorcas turned to the couple on the sofa. "When was the last time you fed her?"

"Ummm," Brittany said.

"What we do with our kids is our business," Kevin said.

"You just made it our business, buddy," Paul said.

"It's not my fault," said Brittany. "I've got post-partum depression. I need medication." By the sound of her slurred speech, Brittany was already self medicating. "Maybe you could get the doctor to give me something when you bring her back from the hospital."

"You don't get it, do you?" Paul said. He scooped up the dirty little boy, who laughed and began playing with the badge on Paul's shirt. "These two are going into foster care."

"Like hell they are," Kevin said, his eyes too bright, his pupils too large. "We've already been through this before, and we know our rights. You keep your hands off my kids." He lunged at Paul, who sidestepped the attack and quickly set the child down behind Dorcas.

"You stand right here with the nice lady," Paul said, and then turned to deal with Kevin.

"Don't hurt him," pleaded Brittany. "He didn't mean nothing by it." Dorcas saw Brittany's plump hand creeping to her cheek to cover the faint bruise there.

"That's my baby," Kevin yelled, rushing at Dorcas. Instinctively, she clutched the baby to her chest, hearing its pitiful mew of anguish at the pressure of her touch.

And then the baby was torn from her arms, Dorcas's mouth opening in terror as she saw the wizened head flop on the neck too weak to support it. "What you going to do now, big man?" Kevin grinned at Paul. Dorcas heard the siren of the ambulance nearing the apartment building. Quietly, she took the hand of the little boy, who stood with tears running down his grimy face, but making no sound.

"I'm not going to do anything," Paul said in a low, even voice. "You're going to walk that baby to the ambulance and let them help her."

"Doesn't appear to me you're in a position to be giving orders." The baby lay limply in his arms

"Please." Dorcas tried to hold her voice steady.

"Show us what kind of father you are." A rescue worker had appeared at the door, but didn't enter.

"Right," Kevin said. "And give Junior Trooper a chance to jump me."

"I'm not going to jump you."

"Scout's honor?" Kevin laughed.

"Scout's honor," Paul answered, as serious as Dorcas had ever seen him.

Kevin stopped laughing. "It's a deal." He stepped forward and thrust the baby at the EMT. In an instant, Paul had him face down on the floor, cuffing his hands behind the back.

"You said scout's honor." The filthy carpet muffled Kevin's voice.

"I never was a Boy Scout," Paul said. "But I was in 4-H. I got a lot of experience with manure."

Dorcas led the little boy down the stairs to the rescue squad vehicle, where the driver was shutting the door. "Will she—" But then she couldn't finish the question, not in front of the baby's brother.

"Not unless someone's reserved a miracle for her." The driver headed for the cab. "I got to get going."

The little boy started crying. "Sissy," he sobbed. "Sissy."

Dorcas stood staring at the baby through a glass partition. Tubes and patches enveloped the little body. Incredibly, she was still alive. The tenderness Dorcas felt for this tiny fighter welled inside her until she wanted to sob its release, but her professionalism held her back. *From pain rises love*. She shook her head. She didn't have time for this nonsense.

Walking down the hallway, she saw the foster mother and little Simon at the nurses' station and stopped to greet them. "They'll have to teach me how to manage that feeding tube," said the foster mother, who looked too scrawny to feed herself.

Dorcas turned in disbelief to the woman, to ask if she really thought that tiny bag of bones and tissue would ever leave the hospital, but she remembered the little pitcher with big ears. "You have a lot of faith."

"That's about all I got," said the foster mother. "But it's enough."

On her way out, Dorcas saw Paul sitting in the hospital cafeteria, cradling a cup of coffee. She hesitated, then walked over and sat down at his table.

"Hey," he said.

"Hey."

Paul pushed his cup away. "You're the one that told me everything happens for a reason. You want to explain to me how this is God's will?"

"I can't." She began stacking the unused creamers.

"What, you don't have a tract to give me?"

To her horror, the tears she'd been holding back began spouting down her face.

"I'm sorry," Paul said, starting to take her fidgeting hand, then stopping. "It just gets to me."

"It gets to me, too," Dorcas said. "Did you know Brittany is expecting again?"

"Things just go from bad to worse, don't they? Sometimes I wonder if I'm cut out for this job."

Dorcas grabbed a paper napkin from the metal dispenser on the table and mopped her face. "You're exactly cut out for it."

"And how do you figure that?"

Because a man who wears a badge and carries a gun ought to have a tender heart, she wanted to say. "Because you care. If you didn't care, you'd just be a bully with a gun." She crumpled the napkin in her hand.

"I could say the same about you," Paul said.

"Except you'd be a bureaucrat with a clipboard." He pulled his cup toward him and took a sip. "That'd be even scarier." He looked at her and smiled. "Are we OK now?"

"Yes," she said, smoothing the napkin before her on the table. "I guess we just weren't meant to be."

"That's different than saying it's God's will."

"Maybe so," Dorcas said.

Leaving the cafeteria, she decided to look in on the baby just once more, and found the foster mother and Simon gazing at the baby through the glass divider. "Sissy!" Simon waved. "Sissy!"

"Sissy can't wave back," the woman said. "She's just a baby. But she's glad her big brother came to visit her."

"I don't know how you do it," Dorcas said. "Getting so attached, and then not knowing what might happen." Brittany and Kevin already had filed a suit against the department, claiming violation of their parental rights.

"I just love them and let tomorrow take care of itself," the woman said. She smoothed Simon's shining, clean hair. "I don't know how you do it."

"Do what?"

"Go into those situations, deal with those people. I couldn't handle that."

"All I know is that I have to try," Dorcas said. "Somebody has to care enough to try."

"That's what I tell people. Somebody has to care."

Dorcas turned back to look at the baby, who lay with her eyes closed, her face troubled. *From pain rises love.* Dorcas didn't get it. She would never get it.

"Sissy!" Simon waved again.

His voice couldn't penetrate the glass, but Dorcas saw the baby's eyes open briefly, then close again. The little face seemed to relax, just a little, as though she'd found a bit of comfort. *I dwell here.* Of course.

The Caretaker

Edna Simmons sat in an ancient upholstered chair with Tabitha on her lap, slowly brushing the old cat's dark stripes. Poor Tabitha couldn't groom herself very well any more. Edna couldn't, either. She wished she had someone to scrub her back, like she had done for her mother. With the lightest pressure, Edna stroked the gray-tipped hairs. When her mother had become too weak to care for herself, Edna had brushed her hair, too.

Tabitha raised her head, indicating the desire for a chin scratch. Edna set aside the brush and gently tickled the soft fur, still as downy as the day Edna had found the scrawny orphan camped out in front of the door to her brick home, as though the welcome mat were a personal invitation. It had been a misty April day like this, nature swaying between winter and spring, a few sprightly green leaves shimmering next to sodden gray branches.

Edna's fingers worked their way behind Tabitha's ear and the cat raised her head in beatific satisfaction. Edna had been catering to the needs of others her entire life. She'd been the one that stayed home to look after her mother and father, giving up a chance to have her own family, or perhaps teach. Girls used to make those kind of sacrifices.

There was no one to look after Edna. She already had envisioned that she'd probably fall and end her life on the cold pine floor. Edna just hoped the fellows from the funeral home next door would find her before she bloated too badly. The standard-sized casket would be a tight fit, anyway; she couldn't afford any additional fluid buildup.

Her aching joints demanded a shift in position. As

Edna moved, Tabitha rose and stretched, arching her spine. Suddenly, she collapsed back onto Edna's lap, lying limp. "What's wrong, girl?" Edna stroked the cat's head, but Tabitha did not respond, breathing in shallow swallows. Struggling to rise, Edna held the cat to her chest, ignoring the pain in her knees. "Hang on, girl, I'm going to get you some help."

Grabbing her coat, Edna hurried out the door and to her car as fast as her arthritic knees allowed. She cradled Tabitha in her lap, trying not to panic at how Tabitha just stared at nothing, her stripes faintly rippling in rhythm to her fading respiration. When the car stopped and Edna lifted her to carry her into the vet's office, she mewed once, faintly. Then the shallow breathing ceased.

Edna rushed into the building, past the receptionist and into Dr. Hodge's examining room. Instead of Dr. Hodge, she found a stranger in a white coat about one size too big, and a young woman with a slobbering golden retriever. "Get that dog out of here," she commanded. The startled girl obeyed and Edna carefully lay Tabitha on the shiny steel table.

"You can't just—" the doctor began.

"Do something for her," Edna ordered. As the vet gently examined Tabitha, Edna recounted the symptoms.

"She probably had a heart attack," he told her. "She was a very old cat."

"Do CPR! Hook her up to one of those machines. Where's Dr. Hodge, anyway?" Edna doubted whether this young fellow was a real vet. Probably a student, practicing on her Tabitha.

"She's gone."

Edna looked down at the still form and knew the truth. She closed her eyes, overcome by the image of her mother reaching to her from a hospital bad, begging her to yank the tubes that prevented her soul from flying to

Edna's father. *"Let me go. Why won't you let me go?"* Her knees started to give way, but the vet caught her. "Let's sit in the waiting room."

"No, I'm going home." Her hand reached out to Tabitha, to extend one last comfort, but she withdrew it. Spirit no longer resided in that furry husk.

"Would you like any special arrangements? There's a new pet cemetery—"

"No," Edna said. "I don't want any part of that foolishness. She was just a stray that took up with me." She moved to the door. "I need to get home. You send me the bill."

Edna hobbled to her car, then dug in her purse for a tissue. It was ridiculous to cry over a cat. Critters got old and died. That was the way of nature. She sniffed, started the engine and began driving home, turning on her lights and wipers to make her way through the veil of spring mist.

The flashing blue strobe ahead prompted her to slow her pace to a crawl. She saw Officer Paul Goshen standing beside a blue Cadillac. What she didn't see was a ticket book in his hand. The young officer was notorious for letting speeders go with nothing more than a warning.

She drove on, dreading the return to her empty house. With the light spray of rain obscuring her view, Edna peered at an obstacle lying on the highway. Probably a fawn. The deer had overrun the county, and the pests were particularly bad about romping across these rural roads. No, it was a dog. She'd call the highway department when she got home and report the carcass.

Then she saw the head move, just a little. Without thinking, she pulled over to the side of the road, next to a purple clump of flowering redbuds. But she remained seated at the wheel. What in the world could she do for this poor creature? *"Why won't you help me?"* her mother had cried. *"Why do you want me to suffer?"* Edna turned off the engine and stepped out of the car. She should have brought her raincoat, not her winter wool, which she left in the passenger seat. She opened the trunk, rooted around for the tire iron and walked over to the knob of matted brown and white fur.

It would be a kindness to put the dog out of its misery. But she couldn't bring herself to raise the tire iron. It had been too long since the family had moved from the farm to town, too long since she'd helped her mother wring a chicken's neck to fix Sunday dinner, too many years since she'd watched her father butcher a hog. The county had just decided it could no longer afford an animal control officer, but since this stretch of road lay inside town limits, maybe that young policeman could detach himself from the Dairy Queen long enough to do the job that she couldn't. Just then, the dog raised its head and thumped its tail. "I'm too old for this," Edna said, but she bent and gathered the wet and bloody beagle in her arms.

She couldn't straighten. Her knees would not cooperate. She squeezed the little dog as she struggled and he moaned his hurt. "Lord," Edna said to the ground, "I'm ready to drop this burden. If you've got a use for this dog, I'm going to need some help." Edna's faith had dimmed to near resentment during her mother's tortured illness, but now she found herself rising and holding on to the dog.

Wobbling over to the car, Edna shifted the limp weight to one arm. She opened the passenger door and clumsily slid the dog onto her coat, her good woolen coat, instantly ruined by wet dog hair and blood. The dog whimpered when Edna settled him on the seat, then lay still. He'd probably die before she got him to the vet's, but she couldn't have walked away from him. *"Don't leave me, Edna,"* her mother had said each time an exhausted Edna rose to go home and have a bite of supper and rest. *"I want you with me when I go."*

Once more, she stood before the young doctor. "Do I have to pay just because I brought him in?" she asked. "He's not my dog."

"There's no tag," he said. "Someone has to take responsibility."

"Does it cost more for a dog than a cat?"

"Does what cost more?"

"You know . . ." But apparently he didn't know. "To put it to sleep."

"There's no need for anything that drastic. We're going to have to amputate that leg, but he'll recover."

Edna looked at the wrecked form before her. The beagle's brown eyes gazed right back at her, and the tail thumped.

"Call us in a couple of days and we'll tell you when you can pick him up."

"Young man, I have tried to do an act of kindness here, but I have no use for a dog." Edna walked out and went straight home.

The sight of Tabitha's water and bowls assaulted her when she entered her house. She should empty them and throw them in the trash, but she hesitated. Tomorrow would be soon enough.

The next day, Edna called the vet's office. Perhaps the dog's missing owner had shown up. The assistant answering the phone said no one had claimed the dog.

"So what happens if no one comes for him?" The dog would be taken to the animal shelter and, with any luck, someone would adopt him. Edna knew no one would adopt a three-legged dog. She would have shown more mercy by using the tire iron. None of her business now, though.

Edna emptied Tabitha's bowls, but instead of throwing them away, she wiped them clean and set them back on the floor. The reminders would have to go, but not today. She started coughing, hacking until tears spewed from her eyes. That's what she got for standing in the damp cold without a coat, tending to someone else's pet.

She called the vet's office the following day. The dog might have taken a turn for the worse. Maybe gangrene had set in and finished him off. Or maybe his owner had claimed him. No, the assistant told her, he was doing great, but no one had come looking for Beagle Bailey.

"Beagle Bailey?" Edna asked, confused.

"That's what we named him," the assistant said. "You know, like the cartoon, sort of."

What a ridiculous name for a hunting dog. Edna hung up the phone. If they were so fond of him, one of them could take him home. She knew they wouldn't, though. There were too many animals for one vet's office to adopt them all. Well, she certainly couldn't adopt every pitiful creature that crossed her path.

Yet somehow Edna found herself a few days later driving once again to the vet's office, and returning with a limping beagle. He immediately set to sniffing the perimeter, nosing out a catnip-filled toy mouse from a corner. Edna filled Tabitha's water bowl and the dog immediately came over for a slurp, then looked up at her, grinning.

"I guess you want something to eat. All I have is cat food." She shook some kernels in Tabitha's other bowl, and the dog ate it all. He followed her as she made her way to her chair to give her knees a rest. He settled on his haunches and stared at her. "If you want something else to eat, you're just going to have to wait."

She saw Tabitha's brush lying on the little reading table by her chair and grabbed it, determined to start clearing out these useless reminders. Beagle Bailey got up and smelled the brush with interest. Tentatively, Edna applied the brush to the back of the dog's head. He sat there patiently as she worked around his neck and began gliding the brush down his spine. When she reached his hindquarters, he began growling, then snapped at the brush. He quietened the moment she released the brush, but Edna struggled to stand, scolding all the while. "I knew this was a mistake. I can't have a biting dog." She held on to the chair, waiting for her knees to start working. "You've got to go."

The dog flopped to the floor and dropped his head in shame. "You get right back up," she demanded, but the dog wouldn't look at her. "Up," she ordered. This time, Beagle Bailey thumped his tail, but he still wouldn't raise his head. Edna sat down again. What now? Maybe she could get a couple of the men from the funeral home to come over. Or she could call that young police officer. He spent half his time in the mortuary's parking lot, anyway, gnawing a hamburger when he should be stopping speeders.

Beagle Bailey opened one eye to peek at her. "Passive resistance," she said. "I remember that Ghandi fellow pulling that, too." She viewed the three-legged wretch sprawled awkwardly in supplication. He hadn't actually bitten her. It occurred to her that the poor critter probably was still in pain. Her mother had slapped the brush from her hand once. *"You're hurting me! You can't do anything right!"* Even the sight of Edna's tears had failed to produce an apology. *"You don't know how I suffer."*

Those foolish tears fell again. "I did my best," she told Beagle Bailey. "Shouldn't that be good enough?" In answer, the dog rose to rest his chin on her knee, his brown eyes shining in sympathy. "I believe you might be a pretty good dog. You belong with a family that has children, not some old woman." Beagle Bailey thumped his tail.

She stood again and willed her knees to move her to

the door. She opened it to discover that she was in luck. Officer Paul Goshen sat in his cruiser in the funeral home parking lot, snacking as usual. Beagle Bailey followed her outside. Maybe he'd just take off, an act of fate she couldn't control. Instead, he limped along beside her as she made her way to the police car. Let that young fellow earn his keep for once. She had no business with a dog.

"Hey, Miz Simmons." Officer Goshen spooned the remains of a Dairy Queen Blizzard. "If you plan on keeping that dog, you're going to have to buy a license and provide evidence of rabies vaccination."

"This is not my dog," Edna said. "He's just a stray."

"I guess I could drop him at the shelter," Officer Goshen said. "They'll probably have to put him down, but I don't reckon the poor guy has much of a life, anyway."

Edna was revisited by the image of her mother, thin and worn, but smiling after being coaxed into drinking a little hot tea. *"This is a good morning."* Edna frowned at the officer. "Young man, all life is precious."

She turned to reconsider Beagle Bailey, but he was following every dog's birth-given compass that pointed to the road, defying the logic of his recent experience. Even on three legs, he'd already reached the yellow line. Bending to clamp a piece of paper trash in his mouth, he seemed oblivious to the green Jaguar whizzing down the highway.

"Beagle Bailey!" Edna screamed. The dog turned to her without moving, wagging his tail. Edna covered her eyes, hearing the squall of brakes and waiting for the smacking sound of dog flying through the air. But all she heard was Officer Goshen saying, "Wow."

She opened her eyes to see the Jaguar stopped just inches from the oblivious Beagle Bailey, who now began loping toward her. The white-haired man behind the wheel waved and drove on.

"I thought you told me that dog was a stray," Officer Goshen said.

"He is."

"But I heard you call out a name."

Edna went on the offense. "What are you doing wasting time when you ought to be catching that speeder?"

"Oh, right." Officer Goshen stuffed the Blizzard cup into the Dairy Queen bag, knocked the keys out of the ignition, fumbled for them on the floorboard, then took off. Beagle Bailey barked after him, dropping the piece of paper from his mouth. Edna retrieved it with a grunt. A coupon for denture paste. Beagle Bailey grinned at her with pride.

"We're going to have a talk about this road business," she scolded. The dog lowered his head in remorse, his tail drooping. She spoke again, forcing the reproach out of her voice. "But I appreciate the gesture." Beagle Bailey raised his head and wagged his tail. She started for her house, Beagle Bailey limping by her side. "We'll just have to do the best we can."

Going to the Chapel

"What do you mean, you can't find the ring?" My blushing bride burned as brightly as a sun scorched tomato.

"I know it's somewhere here." I dug through every pocket I possessed.

Reverend Aron and his wife, Cilla, our witnesses, stood patiently in the inner sanctum of their church. Actually, there is no outer sanctum in the Wee Wedding Chapel, which is supposed to be a miniature version of a Vegas venue.

I hate to admit this, but the Wee Wedding Chapel was my idea. I couldn't handle the pattern picking and all the rest of the formal wedding drills that Dorcas had been determined to pursue. "What say," I suggested to LizBeth one evening as we shared a banana split at the Dairy Queen, "we just have a simple ceremony and save our money for the honeymoon?"

"Are you kidding?" LizBeth looked particularly alluring in a tank top and shorts. "No ring bearer, no flower girls? No maid of honor carrying the train of my white wedding gown?" She paused. "I like it. Let's do it." Dorcas would never have considered such a spontaneous act. It's what I love about LizBeth. She told me she wanted the honeymoon to be a surprise, and that's exactly what I planned to deliver.

The Reverend Aron rocked back and forth on his feet while I excavated the pockets of my one dress suit.

"Perhaps we could provide assistance," the Rev suggested. "Cilla?"

Cilla glided over to a cherry armoire and withdrew a tray of rings that she extended to LizBeth. "Pick one that you like." With their dark heads bent together over the offering, they could be sisters, except the Mrs. Rev's hair was piled like a hornet's nest and I'm pretty sure the color came from a beauty shop transaction. Also, Mrs. Rev was wearing something pink and frilly that looked like a doll's getup. LizBeth wore a snug black dress that I figure the store intended for a cocktail party. Seeing her in the outfit, though, I had no complaints. They didn't look a thing like sisters.

I coughed and tried to find a delicate approach to the subject worrying me. "This is a loaner, right?"

Mrs. Rev looked at me in shock. "We wouldn't dream of insulting you with such a suggestion."

I spotted the little white tags, prices face down. "Hey, maybe it's in the glove compartment. I'll just go check." These lightning-fast reflexes make me the superior police officer that I am.

Then I saw LizBeth give me a look that could reverse global warming and I knew it was time to fold, so I said, "You like that one, do you?" She'd tried on a gold band with fancy filigree that probably cost extra for each curlicue.

"I do," she said.

"Ummm." Yet another tricky subject arose. "Do you folks take plastic?"

"No problem," said Mrs. Rev, trotting over to the same armoire and returning with a credit card imprinter and sales slip.

Finally, we were duly wed, buckled into the Eclipse and ready to begin our lives together as husband and wife.

"Paul, you missed the interstate ramp," LizBeth said.

"Never intended to get on it. I got something to show you." I turned down the next street and stopped in front of our honeymoon cottage. It was a plain frame house that could use some work, but a man could start a family here, with one or two kids, maybe a pet turtle. No dogs, though. Dogs are too much trouble. "Here we are," I said. "Home sweet home."

"What?" LizBeth stared at the house, but the surprise was on me. "Oh, no. No way."

"What's wrong?" I had to allow that in mid-August, the house wasn't making its best presentation. The grass had grown weedy. The exterior hadn't been massaged by a paint brush for quite awhile, either.

"We already went into debt together to get this car. You're not tying me down with a mortgage. No way."

"I thought you'd be happy." This grand gesture wasn't turning out at all the way I'd planned. I'd kind of pictured myself like one of my ancestors, sweeping aside a bunch of brush to reveal the entrance to the perfect cave.

"Happy to be saddled with debt? Happy that you made a decision for both of us without even bothering to ask me?"

"I just wanted to surprise you." That much, I had accomplished.

"So I guess there's no honeymoon trip."

My policeman's instinct activated, warning me that the next surprise might not go over so well, either. "That depends upon your definition of trip." Before she could speak, I fired up the Eclipse. "Let me just take you there."

LizBeth spent most of the ride twisting the substitute wedding ring on her left finger. I was still trying to remember where I could have stowed the first ring when we arrived at the State Fair of West Virginia.

"This is a joke, right?" LizBeth looked as though she could cry and spit fire at the same time.

"No joke." I eased the Eclipse over what Mrs. Travers might have called the undulating rills of the field that had become a parking lot. When we stopped, I leaned over LizBeth —she smelled good, some mixture of sweet spices — and popped open the glove compartment box. I grabbed two tickets and waved them before my bride.

"Brad Paisley. Box seats." At the state fair, that meant folding chairs instead of the bleachers, but still.

LizBeth started laughing.

"What?" I asked. "You love Brad Paisley." You got to love a guy that names an album *Mud on the Tires*. Plus, he had the added appeal of being a native West Virginian.

"It's just that I thought your surprise was going to be—" She stopped and shrugged her shoulders. "Never mind."

"Come here." I reached for her, risking rib injury from the gear shifter, and gave her a kiss. "We'll go to the show, watch the fireworks, then make some fireworks of our own. How does that sound?"

"It sounds to me like you've already turned the bear loose."

I figured that was one of those metaphors Mrs. Travers used to yammer about, but I didn't worry over it. I set out to show my girl a good time. I snuggled with her on the Ferris wheel. I bought her a candy apple. I won her a huge stuffed panda at the baseball pitch. So maybe it took $20, but the setting sun blinded me. LizBeth walked around hugging that bear, ignoring the jeans and shorts crowd staring at us in our wedding clothes.

The show was great, the fireworks spectacular. We ran into Rev. Aron and Cilla, who'd changed into slightly dressed-down attire, and mutually consented none of us had ever seen a better concert. An occasional rumble from an approaching storm threatened some serious interference, but never materialized. As my wife and I walked to the parking lot, I was pretty well satisfied everything was working out.

Crossing the pedestrian bridge, I thought to myself that on this night of my wedding day, even the jam of traffic trying to leave the fairgrounds seemed like a scene out of a fairy tale, all those lights glowing like gigantic fireflies. Then a crack of lightning split the sky toward the back of the field, startling me into dropping the car keys. It didn't faze LizBeth, who just kept walking. "Come on," she said. "These shoes will fall apart if they get wet. So where'd you park?"

Good question. "Right about here," I said. We'd already walked past several rows.

"What letter was our row?"

I glanced at the sign nailed to one of the light poles casting its ghostie illumination on the field. "This one." That was my sincere hope. But the Eclipse failed to make itself known among the littering of cars belonging to the die-hards buying one more elephant ear and taking one last ride at the carnival.

"You don't have a clue, do you?"

"No, ma'am," I admitted. "I surely don't."

"Just like buying a house without telling me."

"As I recall, you told me to surprise you."

"That wasn't what I expected."

"So what did you expect?"

"I thought you were going to—" She stopped. "Never mind."

"No, tell me." I was starting to get aggravated. "Obviously, you'd already planned your surprise."

"It's just that I'd left that brochure in the car, and I thought for sure we were going to Nashville to that studio where you can record your own CD." She squeezed the panda. "I still have dreams."

I'd seen the brochure, but I thought it was junk mail she'd dropped. "Babe, I'm—"

"Never mind," she said, cutting me off. "Use the

alarm on your remote."

I pressed the little red button on the key fob. Nothing.

"So, we're lost," said my unhappy camper.

"Not at all," I said. "We just don't know exactly where we're parked."

Then it started to rain. And not one of those sweet soaking rains that make the flowers sigh. This was the kind of summer rain where you look up at the first unexpected drops and suddenly find yourself pelted with bullets of water, the temperature dropping a degree a minute.

"What kind of idiot can't even find his own car?" Maybe this hadn't been the day of LizBeth's dreams, but I didn't deserve abuse. I started to reply with a smart remark when I realized the speaker was another woman.

It was Mrs. Rev, standing nearby with both hands on her sizeable hips, giving the holy man a good raking. "This is a silk blouse. I know it's ruined."

The Rev, drawing upon his years of experience in delicate matters of the spirit, shot back with, "What kind of fool wears silk to a country fair?"

"The kind who doesn't have any more sense than to marry a man who thinks he can wear black socks with navy pants." I should have continued walking and looking for the car, but I had to find out just how much water Mrs. Rev's hair could absorb before the structural integrity of the hornet's nest failed. LizBeth stood like a mesmerized child, the soggy panda dangling from one hand.

"So we're back on that again, are we? One wardrobe malfunction and you're ready to excommunicate me from my own church."

"That's already been done once, if you'll recall the reason we had to leave Houston." Mrs. Rev's saturated hive trembled, then collapsed. Her wail of anguish persuaded me that I should steer LizBeth away before the scene worsened.

Miraculously, the Eclipse suddenly made its presence known. I pointed, then reached for LizBeth's hand. She dropped the panda and we started to run across the field, but the muck claimed one of LizBeth's dressy little shoes. "I can't run in these flimsy things," she said, stopping to extract her footgear.

The next crack of lightning motivated me to sweep my bride into my arms and gallop for the safety of our chariot. I deposited LizBeth inside the car, noticing her shivering. "Hold on," I said.

I popped the trunk and rooted through my cargo carry-all until I found an old quilt. Back inside the car, I handed the cover to LizBeth. "Make yourself a cocoon."

LizBeth draped it around her shoulders, clutching it closed. "You had a quilt in the trunk?"

"Never know when I might come across an accident. Got to keep people warm so they don't go into shock."

She gave me a look like she was just meeting me. "You're a good man."

But I wasn't the kind of man who could trail after my wife from one bar and music festival to the next, hoping one little gig would lead to a bigger one, begging radio stations to play a homegrown CD. Something told me the Big Break would be her heart, not her career.

"See what else I found." I held out a little box. "I stored it where I knew I couldn't lose it."

"Was lost, but now am found," LizBeth sang softly as she switched rings, closing the counterfeit in the box.

"You know, if you want to sing, there's the Hope County Chorale," I said. "They perform at Carnegie Hall."

LizBeth stopped singing. "I presume you're referring to the Carnegie Hall in Greenbrier County."

"Well, yeah, but it's still Carnegie Hall." There's

sparkle even in just a drop of a dream.

"Isn't Dorcas in that chorale?"

"Well, yeah," I said, figuring that was the end of the discussion.

But LizBeth smiled in a way that reminded me of a fox finding the door to the chicken house standing wide open. "I'll think about it."

I pointed to the box.

"We can save that for our firstborn's wedding." I could picture that future, with me giving my dad's military insignia to my son.

"Who says there'll be any issue from this union?" she asked. But she opened the blanket, and it was worth the pain of a gear shifter impaling my thigh to accept her embrace.

Glad Tidings

"Daddy, how old is Santa Claus?" Annie sat on my lap, flipping through a picture book about a naughty monkey.

"I reckon he's about two hundred years old." I turned the page to show the little monkey looking very sorry for stealing his brother's bananas.

"How can Santa bring me a puppy if we don't have a chimney?"

I shut the book. "Santa has a magic key and can let himself in the front door. But Santa knows you're too little to take care of a puppy." It was all LizBeth and I could do to keep up with Annie, much less a four-legged critter.

Annie got that look on her face that said superior willpower could overcome a mere daddy's objections. She slid off my lap and went over to the coffee table to check the spread she'd laid out for Santa — sugar cookies and milk, plus a bowl of water and carrots for the reindeer. She worried about the cookies being store bought, but she had an ace in the hole: chocolate milk, which she knew would win Santa over when he read her list.

"Maybe I should tell Santa that a cat or a rabbit would be OK, too.

"Or—" Here a look of frightening female cunning crossed her face. "You're an Awful Sir—"

"*Officer*, Annie."

"Awful Sir," she agreed. "You could get on your police car radio and tell him."

"Don't you worry about Santa — he'll take care of you." She'd love the play kitchen I had just liberated from layaway. My sister had always wanted one, but my mom could never afford it. I bought Annie the deluxe model, not some cheap plastic outfit, but real wood, made in America. I'd worked a lot of overtime to buy the set with stove, refrigerator, range, microwave, sink, dishwasher and cabinet.

Just then, LizBeth came dragging in from work. "What is that child still doing up?" She turned to Annie. "Santa won't come unless you go to sleep." Annie flew off to brush her teeth and put on her pajamas.

After checking to make sure Annie really was in bed, I went out to the truck and hauled in the kitchen set, neatly contained in one big cardboard box. LizBeth flopped on the sofa with a beer and watched me pry open the box. "You're not going to try to put that together tonight?"

"Minor assembly required," I read from the box. "Piece of cake."

"Don't expect any help from me. I'm worn out from wiping old people's butts all day and hunting dentures." She took another sip of her beer. "I don't know why you bought that thing anyway. We ought to be trying to make a doctor or engineer out of her."

I wanted to make a smart remark about LizBeth's own career track, but I wrestled with the plastic foam packing for awhile before I said, "Little boys like to play with trucks. Little girls like to play house."

"Is that a fact? Well, I never did." I could believe that. Her free spirit that had seemed so appealing while we were dating wasn't quite as attractive in a wife and mother, and she seemed to be less impressed with me, as well. LizBeth hadn't taken any interest in fixing up our run-down frame house, and I wasn't exactly a handyman. Her idea of a balanced meal was opening at least three cans. If I'd stuck with Dorcas, there'd be homemade cookies baking in the oven, not the dollar-store brand we'd put out for Santa. And Dorcas would have figured out how to deflate the puppy issue. But then maybe Annie wouldn't be Annie.

Fifteen minutes later, I'd finally freed the foam end cap. I flung it across the room and slid the rest of the contents onto the floor. The number of pieces spread before me seemed way beyond minor assembly.

LizBeth stood up. "I'm going to bed. I recommend you giving her the box to play with and taking that pile of plywood back to the store." I didn't answer. Maybe I was facing a little challenge, but it'd be worth it to see Annie's face in the morning.

I picked up the little booklet that had fluttered out of the box: "Carefully line up the pre-drilled holes." Right away, I discovered that the master carpenters at the factory had sent me two panels that would not match up. I didn't own a drill, but maybe I could hammer the pieces together. I went to fetch the hammer, and then I remembered that it was resting above my head, somewhere on the roof. I'd left it there after renailing a wind-torn shingle, and hadn't remembered it again until after I'd returned the ladder to my neighbor.

This was ridiculous. A toy kitchen would not defeat an officer of the law. I unlocked the cabinet where I kept my service revolver. The butt proved perfect for hammering and I was making great progress until I accidentally brought it down full force on my thumb. Santa would not have approved of the language I spewed.

I heard a door open and then the scuffing sound of little slippers. I switched off the light and hurried down the hall. Before I could confront Annie, she pointed a finger and said, "Daddy, if you don't go to bed, Santa won't come!"

"How do you know I wasn't in bed?"

"I could hear you cussing."

"I'm sorry," I said. "I'll get to bed, right after I tuck you back in." I swept her in my arms and dumped her in her twin bed, brushing her fine dark hair out of her eyes.

She giggled then said, "You go to bed, too, so Santa will bring me my puppy."

"Annie, we've been over this. We've talked about how big a responsibility it is to take care of a puppy."

"But I need a puppy." Her little face was serious.

"Why do you need a puppy?"

"In case."

"In case of what?"

For once, Annie didn't just babble. She pulled the covers up to her chin and said, "In case you and Mommy get a divorce."

I wanted to promise her that would never happen, but I wasn't sure I'd be able to deliver. Instead, I said, "Where'd you get that idea?"

She didn't answer my question. "I want something to love me."

I thought only a woman could break a man's heart, but right then mine split. I sat down on her bed and hugged her to me. "No matter what, Mommy and I will always love you."

Annie whispered, "But I need something all my own." Then she untangled from me. "Go to bed, Daddy, so Santa can come."

I went back to the mess I'd left. If it wasn't midnight, I'd buy the first dog I could find. Then I thought about the beagle that hung around the funeral home. True, he was middle-aged and only had three legs, but that ought to make him easier to catch. Technically, Beagle Bailey belonged to old Miz Simmons, who lived behind the funeral home, but she ignored the leash laws and county dog tax, so I figured he was up for grabs.

The front doorknob had just turned in my hand when I heard a female voice growl, "Where the hell do you think you're going?" LizBeth stood there in one of my Tshirts. With her dark hair tumbled over her shoulders, she would have looked gorgeous if her glare hadn't been so scary.

I spent a few seconds trying to think up some lie, but I didn't have the energy. "I'm going out to get a dog for Annie."

Now the glare turned to fury. "We've been over this a hundred times with that child. I know good and well who'd end up taking care of it, and I don't need one more creature to clean up after."

"I'm too tired to argue about it," I said, opening the door.

"Paul Goshen, don't you dare walk out of here."

I wanted to slam that door so bad, but I immediately thought of Annie, asleep and dreaming of Santa. And I knew if I turned away that the rickety scaffolding of our marriage would collapse. So I closed the door and said, "Annie told me she needed a puppy so she could have something if we got divorced."

Her face changed instantly from anger to anguish. Now she looked like a little girl herself, sad and lost. "Are things that bad?"

I was surprised she was asking me. "I hope not."

We stood there awhile, assessing each other. Finally, she said, "I just wasn't ready to be a wife and mother and wage earner all at the same time." And she didn't look the part either, standing there barefoot with a too-big shirt slipping off one shoulder.

"I wasn't ready, either," I said. "But here we are."

She wrapped her arms around herself and rested her chin on her chest. I wanted to walk over to her, but then she might start crying, and I never know what to do with a crying woman. But she lifted her head just then and said, "Do it."

"What?"

"Get the dog."

"Are you serious?"

"I don't care if you have to steal one. You get Annie a dog." Maybe we really were soul mates. My body started to move toward her, but she pointed to the door. "Christmas is coming. Go."

I drove the cruiser to the funeral home and cut the lights. Nothing unusual about my patrol car being parked there. I got out of the car with my arsenal — a rope and a laundry bag. I wasn't exactly sure how I was going to use them, but an officer of the law is always quick on his feet. And I was pumped by LizBeth's blessing.

The dog was snoozing on the funeral home carport, but he perked up at my approach and started to growl. Apparently he remembered the time I'd chased him around the parking lot after I caught him marking my car.

"It's all right, boy. Good dog," I said.

The low rumbling growling continued and in the moonlight I could see the short hairs on his back rising and stiffening. That couldn't be a good sign. "It's all right, Beagle Bailey." I squatted and snapped my fingers. "Here, boy."

He lunged, or at least as well as an amputee could launch himself. He knocked me over on my back and started scouting for the softest spot into which he could sink his teeth. But I had youth and poundage working for me and I wrestled him off me and into the laundry bag. Then I sat there, wondering if he would bite me through the fabric before I could get him in the cruiser.

That was when Miz Simmons showed up, wearing a yellow chenille housecoat and carrying a shovel. Miz Simmons was not the kind to call for help, not as long as she could wield a weapon. "Oh, it's you," she said, like she was disappointed. "What's in there?"

"Possible rabid animal," I said. Just another one of

those quick-on-my-feet moments.

Then the night erupted with one of those piteous moans that only a hunting dog can deliver. "It's Beagle Bailey!" Miz Simmons said. "You're smothering him to death!"

I thought I could still carry the charade. "I'm going to have to take him in for testing."

"Take him in where?" she cried. "There's only one way to test a rabid animal. You're not chopping off Beagle Bailey's head!" She raised her shovel and I was sure she was about to spread my brains over the parking lot. Instead, she whacked the shovel on the asphalt, but so close to me that I let go of the bag. Beagle Bailey squirmed out and ran to hide behind the yellow housecoat.

Miz Simmons squinted at me. "How come you're not in uniform?"

"Somebody called me at the house and—"

"Who called you?"

I had to get home. Without a dog, I had to finish that kitchen set. I rose, gathered my dignity as an enforcer of the law and said, "Look, it's late and it's Christmas Eve, so I'm not going to write you up for violating the leash law."

"What—" she started to sputter, but I cut her off.

"No, don't thank me," I said. "But you might want to stop by the courthouse in a few days and straighten out those dog taxes." For a woman with knee problems, she moved pretty quickly. Beagle Bailey followed her, but he looked back once, warning me that our business wasn't finished.

It was nearly two a.m. by the time I arrived home. I got to work right away, inserting screws and wishing I owned one of those rechargeable tools. About halfway through the job, I discovered the reason for two lengths of screws, and not even my brawny arm could make those long screws fit into those short holes. With the help of a beer and silent cursing, I began unscrewing my handiwork.

Finally, I completed the kitchen set and shoved the box in a corner of the living room. I'd do something with it in the morning, before Annie woke up. I crept to the bedroom and crawled in beside LizBeth. Lately, she'd been scooting way over to the other side of the bed, but now she sleepily flung an arm around me and I thought maybe Annie wouldn't need that puppy.

Next thing I knew, bright sunshine forced open my eyelids. I stumbled down the hallway and poked my head in the kitchen, where LizBeth was plugging in the coffee maker. "I don't see any signs of a puppy," she said, but she didn't seem particularly upset.

"Had to abort the mission."

I prepared myself to face more interrogation, but instead she said, "See what your daughter's playing with."

In the living room, I heard Annie giggling inside the kitchen set's packing box. The play kitchen sat undisturbed. I walked around to the opening of the box, squatted and froze. LizBeth hadn't seen what I was witnessing. Our child was crooning to a little field mouse that had wandered in from the cold.

The little fellow seemed content with Annie. And why not? Torn bits from sliced cheese lay all around. "His name is Squeaky," she said. "He's better than a puppy. See?" She demonstrated by dropping Squeaky in the pocket of her pajama top. Squeaky's bright eyes peered at me from the pocket.

I tried to think of what to do. In my experience, the majority of the female gender expressed strong prejudice against vermin. If LizBeth happened upon this scene, I guessed she'd take an iron skillet first to Squeaky, then to me.

Then I smelled coffee and knew it was too late to

form a game plan. I turned around and saw LizBeth standing there, sipping from a mug and surveying the scene. "A cardboard box and a mouse," she finally said. "What a Christmas."

"Santa thought of everything," Annie said. "He brought me Squeaky, and he brought a house for Squeaky."

But it turned out that Squeaky thought he was too good for cardboard, now that he was an indoor mouse. By the time LizBeth was on her second cup of coffee, Squeaky had turned the kitchen set into his personal condominium. And like her mother, Annie showed no inclination to use the microwave or range. Not even to pretend. But she and LizBeth were getting a big kick out of using bits of cheese to teach Squeaky to run the play kitchen like an obstacle course.

I watched them leaning close together, their dark-haired heads almost touching. I heard LizBeth laughing with as light a heart as Annie's.

I'll Always Take Care of You

The old women were killing him.

Joe knew that, but felt trapped by their dependence upon him. "Let their own families help out," his wife urged him. "You've done enough. You've got your own AARP card."

But what was he supposed to do when Ivy Ruskin called to complain about her washing machine hopping? Tell her to call her son two states away? He had just crawled into bed after pulling a 12-hour night shift at the bottling plant, but he crawled back out. Grabbing his wool jacket, he set off from his brick ranch across the road toward the old two-story white frame house, crunching through a light layer of frozen snow.

"Any of my husbands would have known what to do, but I'm afraid to touch it," Mrs. Ruskin said when Joe arrived. She led him to the basement, where the washer thrashed as though possessed by demons. "I'm afraid it'll knock me over and you know I've already got the one bad hip."

Joe stopped the washer, opened the lid and removed a wad of towels. "You've got too much in here," he told her. "You ought to wash the sheets and towels in separate loads." Joe looked around at the wooden shelves filled with glass jars of preserved fruits and vegetables. Many of them looked as if they'd been there for several years, their contents dark and murky.

Mrs. Ruskin clutched her housecoat to her throat as though Joe might take advantage of the situation to survey her sagging, ancient assets. "I hate to waste water."

"And you were never unbalanced before?"

"No," Mrs. Ruskin told him solemnly. "I was never unbalanced before."

Like a magician pulling a never-ending scarf from his sleeve, Joe produced a twisted length of flannel material from the washer. "And you always wash this with your towels?"

"Oh, no, those are new sheets." Mrs. Ruskin beamed. "My son sent those to me to keep me warm. Isn't he thoughtful?" An apartment in an assisted living facility would really be thoughtful, but Joe said nothing. They climbed slowly back up the stairs.

"Did I ever show you Mr. Man?" she asked, pointing to a face jug sitting on the mantle in her living room. Hideous failed to do justice to the brown pot, jeering at him with features that were a grotesque exaggeration of the human face. Mrs. Ruskin had shown it to him at least a dozen times, each time telling him how her son had it appraised and how it was made by a German potter, and that it was quite old, certainly 19th century, and worth — she always whispered here — thousands, and how that was going to be her legacy to her boy.

Usually, he let her tell the tale afresh, though he was skeptical of the monstrosity being worth anything. This morning, fatigue prompted him to interrupt. "Yes, ma'am, you showed me last time I was here."

"Oh," she said. "Let me fix you some breakfast. Big fellow like you needs to start the day right." Still clutching the housecoat with one hand, she smoothed back a lock of hair darker than any shade nature could produce.

"I appreciate the offer, but I'm going back to bed."

"Oh," Mrs. Ruskin said. "Did I get you out of bed?"

When Joe got home, he discovered that Nadine already had gone back to sleep. He undressed and slipped into bed beside her, spooning himself against the warmth of her curves. He was just drifting to nether consciousness

91

when the phone rang again. Automatically, his hand reached out and jammed the receiver to his ear.

"I saw your light, so I figured you were up," chirped Edna Simmons. "I hate to bother you, but I've got a drip in the basement and I was worried the pipe might burst, especially with it being so cold and all."

Miz Simmons' newly adopted dog confronted Joe at the door. After Beagle Bailey barked and sniffed, he wagged his tail and shuffled aside on his three legs to allow Joe entrance. Joe tried to persuade the stout Miz Simmons, who had arthritic knees, that he could check out the drip by himself, but she insisted on accompanying him into the stony cavern that smelled of mildew and neglect. Miz Simmons had worn herself out looking after her father and mother until they died, and it appeared she didn't have much more care to give. A quarter-sized puddle quivered beneath a pipe. "Um, that's part of your central vacuuming system," he told her.

The old spinster squinted upward. "How could that leak?"

Joe pointed to a damp spot around the fitting. "It's not coming from the pipe. It's leaking around the pipe." He went back upstairs, trailed by Miz Simmons. He located the hose outlet on the partition between the kitchen and the living room, but could discern no water source anywhere nearby. He threw his head back and gazed at the ceiling — no discoloration from a leaky roof.

He returned to the basement, but finding no further clues, dragged himself back up the stairs to stare at the outlet. It just didn't make any sense.

"Care for a cup of coffee?"

"Sure," he said, before remembering that Miz Simmons made the most vile-tasting coffee in the county. He followed her into the kitchen, where Beagle Bailey pranced, or at least as best he could on three legs, trying to draw attention to his food dish. Miz Simmons poured Joe a cup of coffee, then opened her pantry to dip a cup of kibble for the dog.

Joe sipped from a chipped china cup, the jolt from Miz Simmons' special blend of black death sizzling along his neural pathways. The steaming brew smelled like roasted potting soil. He tried not to scowl, concentrating instead on Beagle Bailey's attack on his food bowl. In his haste, the beast knocked it against his water dish, sloshing the contents.

The caffeine in his system began tapping a message to his brain. *Water on floor. Bowl next to partition. Outlet on other side of partition.* He pointed to the bowl, glad for an excuse to set aside the cup. "There's your problem."

"Where?"

"That spilled water is leaking downstairs. There's nothing wrong with your pipes."

"It's the water bowl?" Miz Simmons asked, as though surely the resolution could not be so simple.

"Yep. Just set it far enough from the food bowl so your dog doesn't spill it."

"Oh," Miz Simmons said. "Do you think you should check the flooring to see if it's rotting?"

Joe already had picked up his jacket and was headed toward the door, but he stopped. He could simply say that all she had to do was move the bowl and let the flooring dry, but he knew she'd never sleep again for fear her home was crumbling beneath her. And so he descended again to the basement and made a show of inspecting the wood.

Slogging back to his house in the thawing snow, Joe observed the Saturday sun already lighting the bare hills, but surely he could steal some sleep. He entered the house to find his wife in the kitchen, scowling, holding out the portable telephone.

"I saw you coming from Edna's and I figured I'd better go ahead and call before you got busy," said Wanda Talcott. "There's something wrong with my wood furnace. It's burning too much wood. At this rate, I'll never make it through the winter."

And so he found himself in yet another basement, this time staring in awe at a stove that had burned so hotly that its red enamel was baked to a crispy umber. He strode over and bent to discover a gap in the door to the ash pan.

"Did you know this was open?" he asked.

"Oh, that," said Mrs. Talcott. She was dressed for the day, in a dark blue cardigan and pants, and the same kind of rubber-soled shoes she'd worn during her days as a nurse. "The last time I emptied the pan, it wouldn't go all the way back in, so I just shut the door as far as I could. What's going on with Ivy and Edna?"

"They're fine," Joe said, surveying the toasted stove. "You've been feeding as much air to your fire as if you'd left the damper wide open." Resigning himself, he shed his coat and got to work raking the ashes from the recesses of the furnace.

Back upstairs, he began with diplomacy. "You know, that was a pretty dangerous situation."

"I know," Mrs. Talcott said. "I didn't know how long the wood would hold out."

Joe was tired enough to be blunt. "No, I mean you could have burned your house down."

"Just from burning extra wood?"

In his frustration to be understood, Joe spoke more loudly. "Didn't you wonder what happened to your paint? You had that stove burning hotter than Satan's barbecue pit."

"You don't have to shout," Mrs. Talcott said. "I'm not deaf."

"Just promise me you'll make sure that door is shut

tight."

"I promise," Mrs. Talcott said.

She didn't sound convincing to Joe. He tried another approach. "What you need is a propane furnace. Then you wouldn't have to worry with that wood stove."

"And what if the electricity goes out? Don't you need electricity to run the furnace?"

"Not if you install a stationary generator that runs off your propane tank."

"And where would I find the money for all that?"

"You might talk to the folks at the bank about something called a home equity conversion mortgage."

Mrs. Talcott shook her head. "I don't know exactly what that is, but I'm not about to start borrowing money at my age. Chester worked too hard to pay off this house in the first place."

"I just worry that this place is getting to be a burden for you." Joe didn't look at her as he zipped his coat.

"It's lucky I have such good neighbors to help me out," Mrs. Talcott said, plucking lint from her cardigan.

"You know, I might not always be around."

Mrs. Talcott stopped plucking. "I see. It's not the house that's the burden. It's me."

Mrs. Talcott was a sharp old woman capable of scaring small children, but now Joe could hear the tears in her voice. His tongue rushed to erase his words. "No, no, I just meant me and Nadine have been thinking about moving somewhere warmer ourselves when we retire." He always contributed as much of his paycheck as he could to his pension investment fund so that he and Nadine could be comfortable.

Mrs. Talcott sniffed. "My sinuses are giving me a fit." She sniffed again and said, "You're expecting your first grandchild, aren't you?"

"Yes, in three months."

"See what happens when that baby arrives. You won't be going anywhere. If I had a grandbaby, you couldn't pry me away."

Butterfly-shaped imprints in the snow led Joe back to his home. One day, he'd teach his grandson how to recognize rabbit tracks. And by the time the little fellow was big enough to tag along with his grandfather, Joe would be retired and ready to teach the boy the fine art of fly tying. Maybe they'd start with Wooly Buggers. He stepped inside the house to the inviting smell of frying eggs and bacon, a welcome change from his weekday routine of whole-grain cereal and juice.

"You've already put in a full day's work, so I figured you've earned a field hand's breakfast," Nadine said, standing at the stove with a spatula. Joe hung his coat on a peg near the door and headed to the kitchen sink to wash up. He was just plugging in the toaster when Nadine intervened. "Just hold your horses." She turned to the oven.

"No," Joe said. "It can't be." But Nadine did indeed produce a pan of beautifully browned biscuits. "You are a queen among women."

"You got that right," she said, grinning.

"I bet you're the most popular cook in the school cafeteria."

"Not on the days the county makes us serve broccoli with pizza."

Joe seated himself at the pine table they'd bought when they married. "I don't reckon there's butter for those biscuits?"

Nadine opened the refrigerator and handed him a tub of heart-healthy margarine. "Let's not get carried away." She joined him at the table. "I thought after you got some sleep that we might go to the mall today. I've been thinking of picking up a few more things for the baby."

Joe swallowed his bite of biscuit. "Can't. Got to cut

firewood."

"In the middle of winter? How are you going to saw frozen wood?" That little frown that had looked so cute back when they were dating, and she was still a natural blonde, had turned into a wolverine grimace.

"We had that warm spell earlier in the week." He crammed another hunk of biscuit in his mouth, already foreseeing that this breakfast was not going to end happily.

"We've got plenty of wood."

"But Wanda Talcott doesn't. She's been running that furnace of hers full blast."

Joe waited for Nadine to start her harangue about how he never had time for his own family, but she just sat there, disappointment clouding her face. Finally, she said, "I guess I can go by myself," stood up and left the room.

She hadn't returned from the mall when Joe arrived home from his wood-cutting expedition. He made two cold bacon biscuits and sat down with the mail at the kitchen table. The biscuits still sat untouched when she burst through the door, her cheeks bright from the cold, her good mood obviously restored by whatever lay within the bags she was carrying.

"I found the cutest—" She stopped and set the bags on the floor. "What's wrong? Is it the baby? Is it—"

He thrust the letter at her. She sat at the table, read it through and said, "It's all gone? Your retirement's all gone? How can that be?"

"My own stupidity," Joe said.

"But you had it invested through the company."

"Through the company, not with the company," Joe said. "You remember when we talked about how to invest my pension money?"

Nadine turned the letter over as though some clue might be embedded there. "I remember you coming home and talking about having to pick from some funds."

"Remember that we talked about going with the aggressive growth?"

"Sure, I remember." Nadine said. "Who wouldn't want aggressive growth?"

"It looks like whoever was picking the stocks got too aggressive."

"Then the company will have to make it up to you."

"No," Joe said. "That's why they call it self-directed."

"Then the money's really gone?"

He'd spent his best and strongest years working for the freedom in his old age to fish and play with grandchildren. "It's really gone."

Nadine looked at the bags on the floor. "Going right back to the stores, don't you worry." She started to get up, but he laid a hand on hers.

"Nadine." She turned to him with the look the old women gave him, that trusting gaze that he could make it better. "We might have to sell this place."

The expression of trust turned to shock. "But you're working, and I'm working—"

"We still won't have the note paid off by the time we both retire. Social Security checks won't make a house payment."

"Where would we go?" He hadn't seen that fear in her eyes since the time their little girl had broken her arm on the swing set. Even these many years later, he could still hear that cry of pain that sent both of them racing from the tomato patch.

"I don't know, Nadine." He squeezed her hand. "I wish I did." He wanted more than anything to erase the worry from her face. He would just have to work harder.

Now, when he wasn't at the plant, Joe stocked grocery shelves. "No, Joe has to have his supper and then he's due at his new job," he heard Nadine saying one evening when he came in. "Maybe your son can come in and take care of it."

She clicked off the portable phone. "I swear, I think those old women have some kind of radar system rigged to your truck."

"What does Mrs. Ruskin need?"

"Never mind what she needs," Nadine said, setting before him a bowl of vegetable soup. "What about you? You can't keep this up, hardly sleeping—" The phone rang again. "Hello? No, he can't. He has to go to work."

"Which one was that?"

"Edna."

"What does she need?"

"It'll wait." Nadine said. "Eat your supper." She watched him eat, then repeated, with that wolverine frown, "You can't keep this up. I'd rather live in a tent than see you work yourself to death."

Joe ate quietly, trying to figure out when he could stop by and see about Edna Simmons' problem. Whatever it was, he knew she was counting on him to take care of it. He'd have to find time for Ivy Ruskin, too. That son of hers wasn't dependable. Maybe he'd sneak over there when he finished his next afternoon shift at the plant.

He didn't have to sneak. When he got home, there was no Nadine, just a note saying she was still at school and that he'd find supper in the refrigerator. Immediately, he called the school. When she finally came to the phone, he said, "What's wrong?"

"Nothing's wrong. I left you a note."

"Why are you still there?"

"I'm working," she said. The background noises he heard sounded more like floor buffers than kitchen utensils. "I got an extra job helping the janitors." Before Joe could finish sputtering, she said, "I can work just as hard as you," and hung up on him.

But week by week, the strain began to show. Nadine's rheumatism flared. Joe's back constantly ached. The phone had stopped ringing because the old ladies couldn't find anyone home, but any quiet time Joe and Nadine had was dedicated to rubbing each other with medicated ointment.

"You in the mood?" Joe asked Nadine one Sunday afternoon as they sat in their respective recliners in the living room.

"Sure," Nadine said. "Who's going to get the tube, you or me?" The doorbell chimed. "Wonder who that is?" Then she shot to her feet. "Oh, maybe the baby's coming — maybe they're on the way to the hospital!"

Joe was too sore to stir. "I doubt whether they'd make campaign stops on the way."

It wasn't their daughter and her husband. Before them stood the old ladies, all three of them, still dressed in their Sunday church clothes. Joe saw Nadine's face, and knew she was thinking of the unwashed dishes in the sink.

Wanda Talcott didn't wait to be invited in. She stepped right into the living room and seated herself after straightening the lopsided afghan covering the sofa. Ivy Ruskin and Edna Simmons followed, lining themselves up beside her.

"Coffee?" Nadine offered in a faint voice, gathering fishing and cooking magazines from the coffee table.

"That would be nice," Mrs. Ruskin said. "Cream and sugar, if you have it."

"Black," said Mrs. Talcott.

"Me, too," said Miz Simmons. "I like a strong cup of coffee."

While Nadine was in the kitchen, Joe began apologizing. "I'm sorry I haven't had a chance to see about you all," he said.

"You're a busy man," murmured Mrs. Ruskin. "We

understand."

"I don't see why they don't make police officers check on senior citizens," Mrs. Talcott said. "Seems like every time I drive by Dairy Queen, that Paul Goshen is sitting there running gas that I'm paying for."

Nadine appeared with an old wooden tray. She served the women coffee from white porcelain cups that had belonged to her mother and that had spent the past several years secure in the cupboard.

Mrs. Talcott took one drink from her cup, set it down and said, "Have you ever tried Folger's?"

"I'm partial to Dark Peat," Miz Simmons said.

"I like those flavored coffees," Mrs. Ruskin added.

Mrs. Talcott opened her purse, withdrew an envelope and handed it to Joe. "This is for you two, from all of us."

With Nadine standing behind him, peering over his shoulder, Joe opened the envelope to find a bank deposit slip for his and Nadine's account. The deposit was a hefty one, big enough to make mortgage payments.

Joe stared at the women. "You put money in our bank account."

"Yes!" said Mrs. Ruskin, with a big smile.

"Why?" Nadine asked, exhibiting her frown.

"We heard about your problem," Miz Simmons began.

Joe felt Nadine's fingers gripping his shoulder. "You heard about our *problem*?" she said.

"For crying out loud," said Mrs. Talcott. "Edna heard about it from one of those fellows who works at the funeral home, and he heard about it from his wife, who works with your daughter, and besides, you're not the only one at that plant that got one of those letters."

Joe shook his head in puzzlement. "But you don't have this kind of money."

"Home equity conversion mortgage," Mrs. Talcott said.

"But that means there won't be any money left when your house—" Joe didn't know how to tiptoe around *when your house is sold after you die.*

"Edna and I don't have children and our relatives are doing well enough." Wanda picked up her coffee cup and took another sip. "Did I ask you whether you ever tried Folger's?"

"But you have a son," Nadine said to Mrs. Ruskin.

"I sold Mr. Man."

"But that's your son's legacy." Joe had heard her say it enough times.

Mrs. Ruskin shrugged. "He'll have the house."

Joe tried to thrust the check back at Mrs. Talcott. "We can't take this."

"You'll have to," Mrs. Talcott said. "It's already in your account."

"There's no telling when we could pay you back," Nadine said, but from the easing of her fingers Joe could tell she already was contemplating a future without janitorial labor.

"We're not expecting you to pay us back," Miz Simmons said.

"Of course we'd pay you back," said Joe, feeling himself slide from prideful resistance to visions of freedom from lugging cases of bottled water and pallets of canned baby peas.

"If you try to pay me, I'm going to demand an invoice every time you set foot in my house," Mrs. Talcott said. She took another sip of coffee. "This isn't instant, is it?"

Joe protested one more time. "You can't just give us money."

"Regard it as a favor for a favor," Miz Simmons

said. "And as a matter of fact, there is one you can do for me."

"Anything," Joe said.

"I was reading that dogs should have their anal glands expressed, but I think I'll need some help with Beagle Bailey."

Joe had no idea what expressing anal glands involved, and he was pretty sure he didn't want to participate, but it was too late. He was trapped. He had a feeling that he'd been fated for this moment even before his birth. He felt Nadine's fingers massaging his shoulder in sympathy. "I'll see what I can do."

"Oh, and the next time you have a chance to stop by," said Mrs. Ruskin, "I was wondering if you could check out that smell under the house."

Joe was pretty sure nothing good could come of scrabbling around on the dirt of the crawl space. The sticky spider webs would be nothing compared to the touch or smell of groundhog, possum or whatever lay rotting underneath there. "I'll see to it."

Mrs. Talcott stood. "I've got a broccoli casserole I need to take out of the oven." The other women got up and followed her to the door. Just as she stepped outside, Mrs. Talcott turned to Joe. "When you have a moment, I've got a leak in my roof."

That meant a trip to Mrs. Talcott's attic, which was piled with loose insulation, the only foothold the old ceiling joists requiring the balance of a gymnast. "I'll check it out," Joe said, closing the door.

Nadine was holding the envelope. "Is this our deliverance or a visitation?"

"It seems pretty miraculous to me," Joe said.

"I have a feeling you're going to pay a lot of sweat equity for this gift."

"You know I was going to have to find the time to

help them, anyway."

"I know," Nadine said. "Just don't forget about this old lady. After all, I'm about to become a grandmother."

"Don't worry, I'll always take care of you," he said, then brushed his lips against her ear. "I'm going to get the ointment right now."

Beagle Bailey

I'm going to get Police Man if it's the last thing I do.

I hate a uniform. Always have, ever since that van hit me and the man with the cap and striped shirt acted like it was my fault just because I'd been napping in the road. Lucky for me that Old Woman stopped, even if she did deliver me into the hands of another man in a uniform. This one, in a white coat, sawed off one of my legs.

Still, I had it pretty good until Police Man showed up. I'd have my first breakfast, at home with Old Woman, then I'd mosey over to the parking lot to catch the Men In Suits going to work. I could always count on getting a strip of bacon from a biscuit if I sat and grinned. I'm not exactly sure what those men do, but it involves herding people in the building, then herding them back out and stuffing a bunch of flowers in a vehicle and driving off.

The first day Police Man showed up in his car to eat his lunch, I thought he might be all right. He even tossed mc a piece of ham from his sandwich. Then he went nuts just because I marked one of his tires. The car was something new in my territory; I had to stake my claim. But Police Man jumped out, hollering and waving his arms. I wasn't scared of him, but I ran off, or at least as well as I could run on three legs.

Next day, he came back. A new day requires new territorial markings, so I went over to tag a tire. This time, I growled at him when he chased me, just to warn him to park somewhere else if he didn't want to obey the rules. But the following day, he returned. I considered just ignoring him, but I couldn't leave that car unattended.

That was when Police Man let me have it with a blast of water, which I most certainly did not welcome on a day when the ground already was covered with cold, wet white. I've seen Small Ones with little water shooters, but nothing the size of this weapon. "Gotcha, you—" Then his car started squawking at him, and he took off.

Now it was war. But before I could figure out my strategy, he scored again. I never expected him to sneak up on me at night. At the time, I was paying back the Men In Suits for their generosity by guarding their back door. I'd just decided I could afford a little nap when Police Man drove up. He got out of his car and walked right over to me. I growled, just to show him I wasn't going to tolerate any nonsense.

"It's all right, Beagle Bailey," he said. He squatted, just as friendly as could be. "Here, boy."

I saw my opening and went straight for his throat. But my aim was off, thanks to my missing leg, and all I succeeded in doing was knocking him over. Still, I should have had the advantage, but the next thing I knew, he'd stuffed me in a big cloth bag.

This was the end, I knew. Then I heard the voice of Old Woman, asking Police Man what was in the bag. "Possible rabid animal," the liar said. I barked for help and Old Woman answered my plea. I heard the whack of metal on the parking lot, then felt Police Man's grip loosen on the bag. I wiggled out and ran straight for Old Woman, who was holding a shovel. Before I followed her back to the house, I gave Police Man a look just to let him know I wasn't done with him.

I knew I'd escaped a certain death, and I showed my appreciation to the Old Woman the next day by letting her brush me as long as she wanted. I even let her tie a piece of red cloth around my neck. "Bandana Bailey," she laughed, then choked and launched into one of her coughing fits. I just hoped that half-breed German Shepherd wouldn't come nosing around the neighborhood on this particular day. Maybe I'd just hang around the house.

But the Old Woman opened the door. "You'd better be about your business," she said. I thought she'd pat me on the head, but instead she grabbed at the doorframe. "I'm going to lie down," she said. "Go on, now." And she shut the door.

I went about my business, then decided to return to the house before that shepherd could catch sight of me. I scratched and scratched at the door, but it didn't open. Then I started to whine. It still didn't open.

I flopped on the doormat, figuring she was running that cleaning machine. She'd let me in pretty soon. When she still hadn't called me in for lunch, I went next door and got a slice of cheese from one Suit, and a chicken strip from another. I looked for Police Man, but he wasn't around. I went home and scratched at the door. Nothing. Now she must be watching that picture box. I settled down for an afternoon nap, curling up against the cold.

When she hadn't let me in by supper time, I knew something was wrong. I saw a couple of the Suits headed for their cars and limped over to them, barking so they wouldn't leave.

"Sorry, Bailey," said the Young Navy Suit. "You cleaned me out at lunch." He tried to get in his car, but I wedged myself between him and the door, still barking. "Bailey, what's got into you?"

Brown Suit with Bald Head stood looking at me. "I think he's having a Lassie moment. What's wrong, boy?"

I trotted a few steps toward home, then stopped and barked, to show them they were supposed to follow. Humans are pretty dense, but they finally followed me to the door and knocked. After a few minutes, Navy suit knocked again. Nothing.

Brown Suit sighed. "I'll call Paul Goshen. You might as well start making arrangements." And they just walked away. I barked and ran around them in circles, but they just headed straight into their building.

Then that hateful Police Man showed up and went right to my house. I ran over to my door, barking and growling, but the next thing I knew, the men were back and Brown Suit had grabbed me. "Easy, boy."

"I don't suppose a neighbor might have a key," Police Man said.

Brown Suit laughed. "You think she would trust anyone with a key?"

Navy Suit reached in his pocket and pulled some kind of card from his wallet. "I can get us in."

"You and James Bond," Brown Suit said.

After several attempts to poke the card between the door and the lock, Navy Suit reached into his pocket again and tried to use the blade of his pocket knife. Finally, Police Man said, "Step aside, boys, and watch a law enforcement professional." He kicked the door open.

I struggled out of Brown Suit's grip to go warn Old Woman about Police Man. She was stretched out on the kitchen floor, asleep. I barked, but she didn't move, so I licked her face. When she didn't try to swat me away, that was when I knew. Flopping beside her, I started to whine. She'd been so good to me. She could have left me lying in the road that day, or in the den of that white-coated torturer.

When Police Man walked into the kitchen with The Suits, I sat up and warned him with my deepest growl.

"Bailey doesn't seem to care much for law enforcement professionals," Brown Suit said.

"We've got some history," Police Man answered. "I guess I'd better call the shelter."

"Can't you just let him hang around our place?"

Navy Suit asked. "We feed him half the time, anyway."

"No can do."

"You turn a blind eye to plenty of trespasses," Brown Suit said. "When was the last time you issued a speeding ticket?"

"Look, we've already had one incident with him wandering onto the highway," Police Man said.

"You know they'll just put him down," Navy Suit said. I didn't like the sound of that.

"Why don't you take him home, then?"

"Can't." Navy bent to pat my head, and I relaxed, though I kept my eye on Police Man. "Wife's allergic to pet dander."

Police Man turned to Brown Suit. "How about you?"

"You know I'm in an apartment," Brown Suit said. "Hey — you've got a yard and a kid. Why don't you take him home?"

Police Man shook his head. "That dog has it in for me."

Brown Suit headed out of the kitchen. "You guys figure it out. I need to call her minister." I rose slowly. As soon as he opened the front door, I snuck across the kitchen and through the living room, slipping out the door behind him. "Hey—" Brown Suit said, but I was gone.

The lonesome sound of a crying child drew me into a yard, where I found a girl in a pink jacket standing under a pine tree by a patch of freshly disturbed dirt. I sat down politely and wagged my tail. My sniffer got the better of me, and I couldn't stop myself from nosing around. Something delicious and dead lay just beneath the soil, frozen enough so that Little One had just barely scratched enough to cover whatever she was saving.

"No, doggie!" Little One scolded, and I sat back

down. This time, I whined as I wagged my tail.

"Oh, poor doggie, you only got three legs." Little One held out a hand, and I licked it. She giggled at the tickle, and I moved in, nosing her damp cheek. She hugged me, and I wagged even more.

"Squeaky died," she told me. "Mommy said he was just a mouse, and good riddance. She didn't think I heard, but I did." Then she lifted the flap of one ear and whispered, "I'm going to run away. You can come with me."

This seemed like a very bad idea to me. I was hoping to get some supper from the house, then sneak back to this tempting dirt for dessert. I shook my ear from her grip and flopped on the ground to show her that we should stay put.

I couldn't believe it when Police Man's car turned into the driveway. How had he found me? He jumped out of the car and I felt my hair freezing into place. I got up and growled low and deep. This new place had possibilities, and I wasn't leaving without a fight.

"Annie, go in the house," Police Man said, his voice low and deep, too.

"But, Daddy, look at the doggie." Little One seemed to know Police Man.

"Honey, I think there's something wrong with him." Police Man stepped toward us. "Go in the house." I didn't like his threatening tone, so I bared my teeth and growled again.

I didn't mean to scare Little One, but she started crying and backing up. "It's all right, Annie," Police Man said, quiet and slow. "Just walk into the house." I considered following Little One, then I saw Police Man easing a hand into a holster and bringing out a shooter. I stared at the shooter, knowing there was no use running. This was it; he was going to finish me off.

"Daddy, don't," Little One screamed, racing from the doorway to fling herself at me. "He's just growling because he's scared." Her cheeks were wet again and I poked my tongue at the salty tears. "See, he loves me."

Police Man shoved the shooter back in his holster, looking shaky and pale. "Annie, don't you ever disobey me like that again. Do you realize—"

"Daddy, please," she said. "Can we keep him?"

"Annie—"

"Squeaky's gone and I need something to love me."

I sensed an important opportunity. I didn't want to do it, but I crept over to Police Man on my belly. I lay at his feet, whining like a beggar.

"Please, Daddy, please."

Police Man threw up his hands. "All right. I give up. But he stays outside. And—"

Little One rushed to him and wrapped her arms around his knees. "Thankyouthankyouthankyou."

I crept around to the other side of the car and relieved myself. Soon, I was sure, Annie would be sneaking me into the house. I'd find a pair of his pants, or at least a sock, and I'd have my revenge.

I'll get that Police Man, if it's the last thing I do.

Handout

Connie wavered in the cold, willing the church to open, for some angelic soul to step forward and welcome her. She'd tried the front door, then slipped and slid her way through the icy snow to the side door and even to peer into the window of the basement meeting room. Nobody. Knowing she could not go home to her children and her mother empty-handed, Connie tried all the doors again, hammering with her bare fist. Nothing.

Maybe someone at the nursing home across the street could tell her something. Connie started to cross, skidded in the speckled slush and fell. She lay on her side, wondering if she'd sprained or broken anything, but there was no one to help, so she rolled over, planted her hands on the rough asphalt and heaved herself upright. The bulk of her body and her heavy coat seemed to have cushioned the fall, but when she bent again to retrieve the gray knit cap that had flown off her head, she felt a protest in one hip. She straightened carefully, hoping the pain would work itself out.

Stuffing the soggy cap into her pocket, Connie saw that she'd ripped one arm of her good coat. She brushed the dirty sludge from her coat and pants, dragged her fingers through her short dark hair and picked her way to the Gentle Care nursing home. No receptionist occupied the front desk, so Connie tried to catch the attention of a nurse's assistant in pursuit of an old man propelling his walker to the door. "Excuse me," Connie said to the young woman, whose name tag read *LizBeth*.

"What?" the young woman answered, but she rushed past Connie. "Mr. Echols, where do you think you're going?"

"I got a delivery to make." The old man tried to use his walker to push his way through the front door, but LizBeth intercepted him and steered him back down the hallway.

"You don't want to leave without your dentures, do you?"

The old man considered and said, "No, I reckon not."

Connie wondered if she ought to point out that he already had teeth in his mouth, but she only repeated, "Excuse me."

"You need some help, young woman?" Mr. Echols asked. Nature had given him a full white beard to compensate him for the loss of the hair on his head.

"Yes," Connie said to LizBeth. "I'm trying to find the food pantry."

"I don't know anything about a food pantry," LizBeth said, keeping an eye on Mr. Echols, who gazed longingly at the door.

"See, we were flooded out and—"

"I remember that flood," Mr. Echols said. "Drowned pigs bobbing down the road like corks. Train couldn't get through for weeks."

A shriek from one of the rooms stopped the conversation and LizBeth turned to the source of the sound. Mr. Echols took the opportunity to lean into Connie and whisper, "You get me out of here and there's money in it for you."

"Maybe somebody at the nurses' station can tell you something," LizBeth said, pointing down the hall, then steering Mr. Echols into his room before hurrying to attend to the shriek. The squeaking of her rubber-soled shoes grated Connie's already frayed nerves.

Neither of the two workers at the nurse's station

knew anything about the food pantry. They turned back to their task of loading the plastic trays from supper onto carts. The one wearing an institutional tunic patterned with frantic butterflies headed out with a cart for the kitchen, but Connie didn't leave. She'd spent all day being shuttled from one agency to another, and she still had nothing to take home to her family. She simply stood there with the quiet expectation that these people with their multi-line telephones could locate the holder of the key to the food pantry. Like the wheelchair-bound residents loitering at the station, she waited for something to happen.

"I can't eat that starchy food," complained one thin old woman. "I haven't eaten white bread since the modeling agency made me lose ten pounds."

"That's been some time ago," said the aide, a tired-looking middle-aged woman. She wore a tunic printed with bright red poppies. "And you could have eaten the fish."

"Oh, that was supposed to be fish?"

Connie interjected in an attempt to engage Poppy. "We were flooded out. They sent me to that church over there, but it's locked up."

"What flood?" The aged beauty squirmed in her wheelchair. "I never heard about any flood. Are we safe? Has the water been contaminated?"

"Don't you worry, it was just the west end of the county," Poppy said, then turned to Connie. "Who sent you?"

"Welfare." Connie's first impulse always was to respond directly, but she immediately knew she'd made a mistake. The compassion that had begun to show at the mention of flood now disappeared behind a shade of disapproval. Desperate to re-establish the connection, she said, "It's my kids I'm worried about."

"You have children?" This kindly inquiry came from a dumpling of an old woman with a perm that blossomed from her head like a shower cap.

"Yes," Connie said with eagerness. "I got a little girl, seven, another one, ten, and a boy, thirteen. You know boys can drink a jug of milk a day."

"They're not sitting outside in a car on a day like this are they?" the fish detractor said, as though Connie had no better sense than to let a child freeze. "Or out there unsupervised with the motor running?"

The need to win sympathy quelled the anger threatening to flare in Connie. "No, they're going to my mom's after school."

"Why isn't your family helping you?"

Connie swallowed her resentment of the intrusion. She'd learned that she had to give up the details of her life in the barter for assistance, and she knew Poppy was listening. "My mom's been trying to help out, but she's in a bind, too."

Poppy looked at the giant clock on the wall. "Quarter to five. I don't know who you expected to find this late on a Friday."

"I went right to the flood relief office this morning, but they sent me to social services and they sent me to —"

Poppy interrupted her. "Let me try to make a couple of calls." She waved to a small sitting area across from the nurse's station. "You can wait over there."

Obediently, Connie sat down, frowning a little as her hip protested, wishing she could have a cigarette, even if she had just recovered from a round of bronchitis. She was always trying to quit, but then her nerves would act up. She tried to calm herself by taking deep breaths, but the sharp combination of pine-scented cleanser and the musty smell of age-ripened flesh set her to coughing. "One woman, three children," Poppy was saying to someone on the phone. "No, I didn't hear anything about a husband. All right, I'll hold."

"People shouldn't have children if they can't support them," said one of the old men in the wheelchair circle, as though the distance of a few yards from Connie provided a sound barrier.

When Connie found out she was pregnant with Jeremy, she'd been a dumb teen-ager. She was officially an adult when Amber came along, but still dumb enough to think her boyfriend was going to marry her. He'd actually promised a wedding before Kimberly was born.

But Connie, roasting in her ripped coat, couldn't say all this to a bunch of strangers. She couldn't explain how some days, when Amber anxiously reminded Mamaw to take her medicine or Kimberly tenderly bandaged her dolls, she saw them growing into nurses or doctors. Or how she hoped that Jeremy might do worthy work with his hands, even if he was a poor student. He'd kept her car running, cleaning out the flood sludge, washing the mud from the oil pan, changing the oil and transmission fluids, replacing the fuel filter, cleaning and repacking the wheel bearings.

"Why do these people live in flood plains, anyway?" said another fellow in the wheelchair camp. He made it sound as though Connie had erected a trailer right beside a sign warning of high waters.

"Why does the state let developers build anything and anywhere?" LizBeth, passing through, stopped. "You used to be a building inspector, didn't you? But right now," she said, releasing the brake on his wheelchair and starting to push him down the hall, "We've got another soil erosion issue."

The aide with the butterfly tunic returned, loading more trays into the metal cart. Connie couldn't help noticing how much food had been left untouched. It was good, solid, food, too — macaroni and cheese, fish, a fruit cup. But she knew better than to ask for the uneaten portions. She'd learned about systems and channels and had heard the word "liability" many times. "You don't suppose she's trying to work some kind of scam, do you?" the ancient beauty said to Poppy. "She doesn't exactly look to me like she's starving. I would never let myself go like that."

Connie shifted in the chair, trying to settle into a smaller mass. She willed the person on the phone to come back on line, to give Poppy the information that would allow Connie to escape.

"You know, I've got some stuff in my car I picked up on my lunch break," Butterfly told Poppy. "Red leaf lettuce, organic pears, wheat bagels—" Butterfly paused. "But she might not even eat that kind of food. I'd hate to waste it."

Connie could not bear to hear anymore. Without a word, she rose and walked out of the nursing home, trying to ignore the stiffness spreading to her back. It was nearly dark and she could see no activity at the church, but she decided to wait in her car, anyway. Maybe there'd be an evening program and the doors would open for her.

She sat hunched in the cold, not daring to start the engine and waste gas just to run the heater. Somewhere deep inside her, a little girl shivered in desperation for warmth and comfort, but Connie had none to give.

The sound of the passenger door creaking open startled Connie. It was Mr. Echols, hanging on to the door post with one hand, the other braced on his walker. He flung himself forward, dropping into the seat, then shutting the door and leaving the walker on the pavement.

"Step on it," he said.

"What?" Connie said.

"Step on it," Mr. Echols said. "Them revenuers can't be far behind."

"Do they know you're out here?" Connie asked.

"Is it money you want?" Mr. Echols asked. He had

no coat.

Connie got out of her car, walked around to the passenger door and opened it. "I'd better get you back inside," she said. Mr. Echols reached out to slam his door shut, and no amount of tugging on her part could persuade him to loosen his grip on the handle.

She had just gotten back in the car, determined to talk Mr. Echols into returning to Gentle Care, when a police cruiser passed by. It pulled over in front of her, flashing blue lights, and the next thing she knew she was producing her driver's license and trying to explain why an expired registration sticker glared from her license plate.

"And who's this gentleman?" asked the officer, a young man with *Goshen* on his badge. "I'm thinking I've had a run-in with him before."

Connie saw him eying the abandoned walker. "That's Mr. Echols. I was just trying to get him to go back inside."

"Turncoat!" Mr. Echols hollered. Connie saw him searching the crevice of the seat, as though he might find a pistol to fight his way to freedom.

Lowering her voice, Connie said, "He thinks the revenuers are chasing him."

"That so?" Officer Goshen strode around to the other side of the car and yanked open the door. "Mister, your number is up. You can come quietly, or I can plug you right where you sit."

Connie gasped. She didn't think the police were allowed to talk to people like that. But the old man just nodded and allowed Officer Goshen to haul him out of the car and onto his walker. The officer told Connie, "If you promise me you'll take care of that registration first thing Monday morning, I won't write you up."

He was considerably younger than Connie, and she did not have the thirty-five dollars for registration, but she meekly said, "Yes, sir." He shut the door and began to escort Mr. Echols into the nursing home. "Save yourself!" the old man shouted to Connie.

Connie started the car, figuring it would be better to be gone by the time the officer emerged from the nursing home. She saw something sticking out of the seat cushion and pulled at it. Maybe Jeremy really had lost his report card. No, it was just a slip of paper. The street light that had begun to glow as dusk deepened to blackness revealed a twenty-dollar bill, folded in half. Connie unfolded it and stared at the dim image of President Andrew Jackson. Twenty dollars. Just enough to get her family through the weekend.

She couldn't keep the money, because Mr. Echols wasn't in his right mind. On the other hand, if he wasn't in his right mind, he'd never miss it. Her kids needed milk and eggs and cereal. And she didn't care how mean those people talked about her, she was getting herself some cigarettes. Her nerves couldn't withstand life without them.

Clutching the bill, Connie found herself leaving her car and walking to the front door of the nursing home. It was locked, probably standard policy after dark. She pressed the intercom button and identified herself. Before she could explain about the money, a voice that sounded like Poppy's said, "We couldn't find out anything. You need to go back to that flood relief office on Monday."

"But—"

"Ma'am, I'm really sorry, but we're not supposed to admit anyone on the premises who isn't visiting a resident."

"But—"

"Ma'am, I really hate to do this, but I have to ask you to leave."

Connie scuttled away from the door, knowing that Officer Goshen was likely to appear and that she could end up in real trouble. She got back in her car, took one more look at the darkened church and drove straight to the grocery store. Her injured hip protested when the right front wheel hit a pothole, the same one she'd nailed the week before.

In the store, Connie walked stiff-legged down the aisles, favoring the aching hip and wondering whether Mr. Echols had missed his money and if the officer might track her down. Two jugs of milk. Ground beef and Hamburger Helper. Two cartons of eggs. Orange drink. Two boxes of cereal, one chocolate coated, one honey-dipped. Jeremy would eat anything, but the girls were picky on school mornings. It wasn't long before Connie figured she had the twenty dollars spent and she headed to one of the checkout lanes.

She was over a few dollars. "All I got is this twenty," she told the checker, who didn't appear to be much older than Jeremy. With his newly mown blond head, he looked more like a duckling wrapped in a clerk's apron.

The checker picked up the pack of cigarettes. "You want me to put these back?"

"No." Her nerves were shot, and she planned to rip open the package as soon as she reached her car.

"They told us at school they use the same chemicals to make cigarettes that they use to make rocket fuel and paint stripper," the boy said.

Connie ignored him, pointing to the chocolate-coated cereal. Amber was old enough to understand that people couldn't always have everything they wanted. And besides, she'd probably be able to get a food voucher Monday. Probably.

The checker deducted the cereal and offered her a dime and penny in change. "Oh, yeah, and the stuff they use in gas chambers, too," he said.

Out in the parking lot of the strip mall, the groceries stashed in the trunk, Connie sat in her car with the window lowered, hoping to evacuate the odor that Kimberly said made her gag. The first inhalation brought relief, then a cough, then shame. Amber's disappointed face hovered in the acrid air she exhaled, but it was too late now to make the better decision, just like it was too late to fix all the mistakes she'd made in her life. Connie smoked and stared at the wet pavement, observing the mashed remains of someone's thoughtless dump of an ashtray. She heard a car pull up beside her and a door open and shut, but she didn't look up.

"Rough day, huh?" The voice sounded familiar and Connie looked up to see that young woman from the nursing home. Lisa. Liza. LizBeth.

Caught in her indulgence, Connie ground out her cigarette, mixing it with the pulp at her feet. "Could be worse, I guess." At least she hadn't gotten a ticket. Yet. "I don't imagine your day's been a picnic, either."

"You learn to tune a lot of it out," LizBeth said. "Did you find that pantry?"

The impulse to confess about Mr. Echols nearly overwhelmed Connie, but she had no way of returning the money now. "No," she said.

LizBeth took off her gloves, reached into her pants pocket, hesitated, then brought out three ten-dollar bills and held them out to Connie. "I know what it's like to be stuck."

Thirty dollars. Nearly the cost of the car registration. Connie wanted to snatch the offering, but she was too ashamed to move. "I can't take your money. That's almost a day's work."

"I was just going to blow it on a pair of jeans that I don't really need, as I'm sure my husband would be happy to tell you."

"I'm not exactly the best money manager myself," Connie said.

"You're human," LizBeth said. "You're allowed to make mistakes." She forced the money into Connie's hands. "Take it."

"I don't have any way of paying you back," Connie said.

"Some day, you'll do for someone else," LizBeth said. Before Connie could answer, she returned to her car and drove off.

The wind began stirring and plucking at the paper she held. Hastily, she grabbed her purse, pulling out the cigarettes to reach her wallet. After safely depositing the money, she started to drop the cigarettes back into her purse, but instead found her hand crushing the package that mocked her lack of control.

Just as quickly, her fingers sprang apart and she stared in panic at what she'd done. She couldn't get through the weekend without them. She'd take just a little bit of LizBeth's money and return to the store.

Connie opened her purse, then paused and sat for a minute, imagining the running and wiping and carrying LizBeth had done for each of those ten-dollar bills. Connie reached for her wallet, anyway. LizBeth would understand. She'd said herself that Connie was allowed to make mistakes.

The duckling checker emerged from the store, wearing a dark cap and an orange stadium jacket that glowed like a radioactive pumpkin under the sickly white light of the mall's exterior illumination. His stride, jaunty even in his drooping pants, told Connie that he was done for the day. He jumped in his pickup and roared off, bouncing through the same crater in the pavement that had jolted Connie, apparently unaware that his exhaust pipe had been jarred loose.

Watching the tailpipe as it dangled, threatening to detach itself from the departing truck, Connie dropped her wallet and the ruined pack of cigarettes into her purse. She started her car and drove slowly out of the mall lot, carefully steering around the asphalt cavern.

Maybe she didn't have to hit the same pothole over and over.

School Bus

It was like a game at first, being the only one on the school bus.

Adrianna couldn't believe her luck. Her regular driver always walked up and down the aisles to make sure no one was hiding or asleep, but today's driver lit a cigarette, which she was pretty sure was not allowed, and got off the bus. Adrianna didn't care. She didn't like being packed off to school like those poor sheep she remembered from the state fair, stuck in those little rooms, stalls Mommy called them, crying to go home. Nana had said that a pre-school program was just what Adrianna needed, to learn to speak up and get along with other children her age.

But Adrianna wasn't getting along. The screams and squeals and jabbering of her classmates ricocheted around her until sometimes she clapped her hands over her ears to shut out the racket. Instead of speaking up, she grew quieter and that made her strange to the other children, who started to tease her about the small silver streak in her dark hair, calling her skunk girl.

She wrestled beneath the bulk of her coat to unbuckle her seat belt, but she couldn't figure out the five-point restraint that looked just like the ones the race car drivers on television wore. Adrianna considered crying, but there was no one to hear her. Looking out the window, she saw nothing but a bunch of other school buses, and a pile of dirty old snow that hadn't melted from the last storm. Gray clouds frowned at her when she craned her neck to look for the sun. She settled back into her seat, intending to sort out her options, but the bus was still warm and it was so early that Adrianna's eyes began to close. That was another thing she didn't like about school, getting up when it was still nighttime, and having to go outside in the cold.

She dreamed of playing in a field with lambs and their mothers, under a bright yellow sun. It was so quiet — no fussing Nana, no uncles wanting to know if the cat got her tongue, no kids hooting the insult of skunk girl. Then her dream landscape grew cloudy and gray, and snow began to dribble from the sky. The lambs ran to the warmth of their mothers.

Adrianna awoke to a cold bus. It was the kind of cold that made your nose drip and your toes tingle. She was thirsty, and she was hungry. Most of all, she had to go to the bathroom. Even if she got into trouble, she'd be glad now to be pulled off the bus and hauled into the warm school. She wouldn't care if the other kids made fun of her. "Help!" she yelled, just like she'd seen people on TV holler. "Help! Help!"

But no one came. No driver, no teacher, no Mommy. Her shouts rattled around the bus and fell, unheard, to the floor. Finally, she began to suspect that she was being punished. Nana had threatened to leave her behind once, when Adrianna wouldn't budge from a toy store shelf of babies that could giggle, drink juice and even swim in water. Adrianna had immediately abandoned the dolls and hurried after her grandmother, sure that nothing could be worse than being left behind.

Adrianna's gloved hand crept to the coat pocket that held her contraband. Mommy said it was just for Snickers, their cat, and Nana said Adrianna could put her eye out with it. She was just borrowing it, to have something to show the kids and maybe stop them from picking on her. Now, though, it seemed that being left alone was what happened when you took something that didn't belong to you.

Guilt and fear weighed upon her until she began to cry, bawling as loudly as those poor sheep at the fair begging to go home to their fields of clover. Her bladder spasmed and she cried even harder at the shame of having wet herself like a baby. Now she'd be in even more trouble. Then, wiping her eyes and runny nose with her fuzzy pink gloves, Adrianna saw an old woman, older even than Nana, walking down the aisle toward her. The granny was a big woman, and she had to squeeze herself into the seat beside Adrianna. "Feels good to take a load off those knees."

"Take me to school?" Adrianna asked, even though she worried that the old woman would smell her accident.

The old lady rubbed a knee. "That feels better." With her big round face and big blue eyes, she looked like one of Adrianna's dolls, but with gray hair. And a lot of wrinkles. And spots on her hands.

"I'm cold." Adrianna's lips were chapped and her wet bottom already felt uncomfortable against the vinyl-covered metal seat.

"Look at that pretty silver in your hair. Did you know that means you've been touched by an angel? Like this." She stretched a hand toward the silver streak, but Adrianna couldn't feel the touch. The granny leaned back. "I've got to rest these knees."

"How come?" Adrianna had never considered that body parts could need rest. She could kneel forever playing with her dolls.

"I've been out looking for my dog."

Adrianna's mouth was so dry, but talking pushed back the urge to cry. "Mommy has a cat." Snickers wouldn't play with Adrianna, not since the time she'd wrestled him into one of her doll's dresses.

"Cats are nice," the old woman said. "I had a very nice cat. Her name was Tabitha."

"Get off bus now?"

The old lady sat up and rubbed one of her knees over and over in a circle. "I wish that dog would turn up."

Adrianna's gloved finger wobbled in the direction of one of the windows. "Hound dog." A three-legged brown-and-white dog limped through the downy snow, sniffing at the tire of another bus.

"That's Beagle Bailey, the scoundrel," the old woman said.

"Go get him," Adrianna said, hoping to be unbuckled and freed. Her toes felt funny.

"I'm not ready to get up just yet, but I wish I could get his attention. I'm afraid he'll wander off and get lost again."

Adrianna brought out the forbidden object from her pocket, but before she opened her hand, she demanded, "Promise not to tell?"

"Promise."

Adrianna uncurled her fingers to reveal the toy laser pointer that Mommy had bought to give Snickers exercise. The minute Adrianna had seen Snickers chasing the dot of light, she longed to take the laser to school, but Mommy had said absolutely not, and Nana had said the very idea, and that she wouldn't be surprised if half the children in the United States wound up with scorched eyeballs.

"What's a little girl like you doing with lipstick?"

The pointer did sort of look like the kind of metal lipstick tube Nana carried in her pocketbook. Adrianna wanted to giggle, but she was too tired. She clicked on the laser and pointed it out the window, making a dot dance against the metal of the bus that Beagle Bailey was investigating. He looked up at the dot and barked at it. She waved the pointer like a wizard with a wand, and Beagle Bailey barked some more.

"That's it," the old lady said. "Keep it up."

But Adrianna needed to sleep, even if it was cold.

"You hold it," she said, and closed her eyes.

Officer Paul Goshen had been driving the streets and highways of Hope County all day, impressing the citizenry with this new display of dedication to patrol. Actually, he was looking for that wretched Beagle Bailey. If it weren't for his little Annie's attachment to the stray, he would be perfectly content to imagine Bailey wandering into a forest, serving himself up as a panther treat. The ingrate had escaped the chain link fence that had been purchased — in monthly installments — for the mutt's specific benefit. The fiend had just been waiting for the moment when Annie would forget to latch the gate and he could push his way to freedom.

Time for a snack. At the Dairy Queen drive through, he ordered a hamburger, a coffee and a ButterFinger Blizzard. When he picked up his order, some young woman he'd never seen before, and he was certain he would have remembered the chopped red hair and lip stud, handed him a coffee cup and the bag containing his burger. "Where's my Blizzard?"

She looked at him as though he were a freak. "I thought you were kidding. It's winter, you know."

"Thank you kindly for the weather advisory," Paul said amiably, and waited, but she made no move to leave her post. "I'd still like my dessert."

When his beloved Blizzard was finally handed to him, Paul quickly rolled up the car window. The air was frigid and sharp, with the smell of snow on the way. He ate his burger and drank his coffee in the Dairy Queen lot, waving at Goldie Martin passing by in her Cadillac before it registered that she had to be driving nearly ten miles over the speed limit. He hated for his coffee to get cold, so he let her sail on. When he'd finished his burger, he decided to have his Blizzard over at the school bus yard. He doubted

Beagle Bailey could have gotten that far, but a couple of buses had been vandalized in the past few months, so he cruised into the lot, isolated at the end of a lonely road.

Paul found the idiot dog baying at the side of a school bus. He parked his patrol car and got out, leaving the motor running, but Beagle Bailey ignored his whistles. "Stay out here and freeze then," Paul said, turning as though to get back in the car. Reverse psychology apparently did not work on dogs, because he did not hear the pitter patter of little paws running to catch up to him. Paul zipped up his jacket and reached into his car for his gloves, then turned back, bracing himself to attempt to drag Bailey away by his collar. Even though he'd been giving the pest free room and board, there was a good chance the ungrateful beast would try to bite him.

Suddenly he saw a laser beam, jumping against the side of the school bus, wavering, then disappearing. His hand twitched toward his holster, but he stood quietly, scanning for the light's possible source. He couldn't see anybody beneath the buses. Then he saw a dark little head, barely visible at the window ledge. He strode over to the bus, pushed open the door and mounted the steps. A little girl sat slumped, lolling against her harness like a rag doll.

Quickly, Paul unbuckled her and lifted her in his arms. "Wake up, honey," he said.

She opened her eyes and he saw they were glazed, the pupils dilated. "Mommy," she mewed through peeling lips.

"That's right, I'm going to take you to your mommy, but first I'm going to get you warmed up." Paul hugged her tight to his chest and carried her off the bus and to his car, where Beagle Bailey, deprived of his entertainment, sat thumping his tail. "Granny dog," the little girl croaked.

"He's going to feel like somebody's granny when I'm done with him," Paul said. Shifting her weight, he freed a hand to open a trunk and grab a blue blanket. When he opened the driver's door, Beagle Bailey tried to jump in, but Paul shoved the dog aside with his foot, deposited the bundle in the passenger seat and slammed the door. Immediately, he cranked up the heater. Outside, Beagle Bailey whined.

The little girl stared at him with fearful brown eyes. "Take me to jail?"

"No, honey, I'm just going to make sure you're all right, and then I'm going to get you to your mommy. What's your name?"

The child poked a gloved finger out of the blanket and pointed to the back of her neck. Paul found attached to her coat a label that had been hand embroidered with a first and last name. "Adrianna. That's pretty. I'm Officer Paul." He turned on his cell phone, hoping to avoid the circus that surely would result if the police scanner audience heard him calling the dispatcher on the radio. "I got a situation here," he began.

"Left behind," Adrianna said as soon as he had finished his request for an ambulance and parental contact.

"That's right, you were accidentally left behind."

"No." She shook her head. "Bad girl."

Paul's heart contracted. "You didn't get left behind for being bad. I bet your mommy's on her way right now." Paul offered his cup of Blizzard, which had turned soupy. "Try some ButterFinger milk. It's delicious." She obediently sipped from the cup, then sank back in the seat.

Beagle Bailey's muffled whine could be heard outside the car. "Doggie cold," Adrianna said.

"He's got fur, don't you worry," Paul said.

"Doggie sit in car?"

"He's fine right where is," Paul said, just as Beagle Bailey raised the volume of his whimpering.

"Doggie cold," Adrianna repeated. Paul saw tears

on her face, and the next thing he knew, he was shoving the muddy, tail-wagging pest inside his immaculate patrol car. Bailey wriggled right up to Adrianna and licked the tears from her face. "Doggie hurt," she said.

"Where did he hurt you?" Paul looked for scratches, preparing to seize the beast and hurl it back outside. He had begun mentally calculating the potential figures of the liability suit when he realized she was talking about Bailey's missing leg. "That happened a long time ago. He's fine now." Paul coaxed another sip of sweet syrupy Blizzard into Adrianna, adroitly avoiding Bailey's eager tongue.

"Doggie bad?"

Having a daughter of his own, Paul sorted out an interpretation of the little girl's fears. "No, honey, he didn't do anything bad. He got hurt by accident, but somebody found him and took care of him." Paul's elbow deftly blocked the slobbering Bailey as he persuaded Adrianna to take another drink. "You don't have to be bad for things to happen. It's kind of like you getting left on the bus by accident, but I found you, and you're going to be OK."

Bailey's tongue darted out for a taste of Blizzard leaking from the corner of Adrianna's mouth. She scrunched her nose, but smiled a little. "Doggie good?"

It killed Paul to have to say it, but he agreed. "Doggie good." Beagle Bailey turned to him and grinned.

Later, Paul was undecided as to which had been the worst experience, being kissed by Beagle Bailey, or blessed out by Adrianna's grandmother, who seemed to hold him, as a representative of Hope County, responsible for the ill that had befallen the child, no doubt scarring her for life, as well as the fact that the garbage collector always threw the trash can lid in the drainage ditch. But after happily handing Nana off to the rescue squad workers, who apparently were in need of advice on how they'd better not speed because she'd heard about their siren-happy ways, Paul had turned his attention back to Adrianna, who was clinging to her mother. No way he was going to stand by and watch this commotion crush this little girl, burdening her with a fear of abandonment.

"Don't mind all the fuss," Paul told her. "Before you know it, you'll be back in school bragging to the other kids about your adventure. You might become a regular storyteller."

"Adventure?" Adrianna's young mother looked as nearly in shock as the little girl. "I don't think—"

"Adventure," Paul said with decision. "Just like Jack in the Beanstalk. I bet he wished at first he hadn't traded that cow for those beans, but everything worked out OK, didn't it?" He saw Adrianna considering this, then nodding.

"So you've had an adventure, but you're OK now. Right?"

Adrianna nodded. "Doggie go home with you?"

"Yep, the doggie's going home with me." She did not need to know that as soon as her rescue chariot left, Beagle Bailey was going to be stuffed in the back seat, where the criminal element belonged.

"I heard they left you on the bus," jeered the yellow-haired boy who'd first called her skunk girl. Adrianna knew his daddy had been sent to the Big House for stealing foxy cotton from a drugstore — she'd heard Nana say so. But Adrianna couldn't bring herself to throw the meanness back at him. She would have tried to slip away, but the other kids crowded around. Knowing the teasing would only get worse, Adrianna could feel those shameful baby tears threatening to spill. She wished she had the laser pointer to turn their attention from her, but she'd lost it on the school bus and Mommy had said never mind about that. Then she remembered what Officer Paul told her. She did have something to offer. She owned an adventure.

"All day," she said. "I was cold." She noticed the interested glances at her, and something emboldened her to add, "Icicles in bus." She pointed to an imaginary ceiling, then downward. "It snowed on the floor."

"You're making that up," the boy said, but the other kids drew closer to her and Adrianna began to tell of a granny as old as the moon, with a magic wand, and the brave dog, big as a pony, that carried her to safety. She lacked the full range of the parts of speech, but she spouted plenty of nouns and verbs. The more she talked, the more it seemed that an old Adrianna had been left behind on the bus. She was a new Adrianna, and the cat no longer had her tongue. She had a voice. She was a storyteller.

Driver's Ed

Seth gripped the steering wheel of the driver's ed car. Though the day was so cold that snow clouds hovered over the school parking lot, perspiration flowed down his spine.

"You can turn the ignition on any day now."

Seth sat frozen. He couldn't remember whether he was supposed to turn the key forward or toward himself. "I'm just checking the mirrors."

Looking in the rearview mirror, he saw three jeering specters: two boys and a girl, all evil. He tried to obliterate their menace by thinking of them as Winken, Blinken and Nod. Seth was the only one in the class who didn't already know how to drive. Indeed, he was the only one who didn't have a license and one of the few who didn't drive his own car. Winken, Blinken and Nod were cruising through the course just to get a break on insurance rates.

Seth's mother would not allow him to practice in the family sedan. "That's the whole point of driver's ed," she'd said when he had tried to procure the keys as she sat at the kitchen table spread with newspaper inserts. "I can't afford to have you making mistakes in my car." She'd reached out to brush his lank dark hair away from his eyes. "I wish you'd let me cut your hair."

"But the car's a piece of crap," Seth said, trying to steer her back to the issue of keys.

His mother had looked at him in sorrow. "Exactly my point," she said, returning to her clipping of coupons.

Mr. Jarvis, who reeked of some aftershave combination of menthol and diesel fuel, pantomimed the turning of the key. Forward. Of course. "Like I said, any day now." Mr. Jarvis frequently reminded Seth and his classmates that he could be coaching at any college in the state if it weren't for his dedication to them and their loser buddies.

Seth started the engine, moved the gear shifter into drive and pressed the accelerator, dreading the surge of motion that he would be expected to control. The car roared and lurched, but refused to move forward. Maybe something was wrong with the transmission, which he knew had some vital connection with making the car operate.

Had the car been a plant or animal, Seth probably could have coaxed it to cooperate. He once had nursed a dying baby squirrel back to life with little more than an eye dropper, Gatorade and the perseverance to feed it hourly through the night. He had saved his mother's African violet by hiding her watering can. But with absolutely no mechanical aptitude, he could see no way of rescuing himself from this nearly exact replica of hell. Seth wondered if things would have been different had his dad come back from Iraq.

"You might try releasing the parking brake first," Mr. Jarvis said. The chorus in the back seat snickered.

Seth released the parking brake and stepped on the accelerator again. The beast leapt forward and he automatically lifted his foot. As the car balked, Seth realized his error and stepped on the accelerator in determination, but backed off again when the car surged ahead. "Keep your foot on the gas," Mr. Jarvis said, without much effort to disguise his exasperation.

Apparently Seth was the only one in the class who had heeded the statistic in the textbook that said cars were two-ton weapons of death and destruction. Nonetheless, he obeyed and pressed the accelerator. The car barreled down the school driveway toward the highway. The stop sign was fast approaching, but Mr. Jarvis hadn't given Seth further instructions, so he kept his foot steady.

"Brake!" Mr. Jarvis commanded. "Brake!"

While Seth's foot clumsily sought to move left, Mr. Jarvis applied the instructor's brake and brought the car to a halt. A tractor trailer rumbled through the intersection.

"I'm sorry—"

"Never mind." Mr. Jarvis sighed. "Turn right and proceed."

First, the turn signal. Next, look carefully for oncoming traffic. Cautiously, just barely tickling the gas pedal, Seth inched onto the road, the only four-lane highway in the county. How did people handle these metallic monsters with such ease? A river barge couldn't be harder to maneuver. Seth concentrated on trying to stay in his lane without running onto the shoulder, attempting to remember how to use the hood as a means of lining up the position of his vehicle.

"We're going to get run over." This from Nod, whose father had bought her a brand-new SUV.

Mr. Jarvis pointed to the speed limit sign. "You need to stay with the flow of traffic."

Ten-and-two. Ten-and-two. Seth willed his sweaty hands to remain clamped on the steering wheel and tried to force himself to go faster. He couldn't do it, creeping toward the next stop sign. Just three more blocks until they reached Mutt's Mini-Mart, when he knew he could relax. "We'll pull in here and switch drivers," Mr. Jarvis would say, meaning that he would take the opportunity to smoke and buy lottery tickets.

Ten-and-two. Ten-and-two. Seth rolled right through the intersection, unaware of his sin until Blinken shouted and horns began blasting. Seth ventured a peek in the rearview mirror and saw blue lights flashing.

"Busted," Winken announced.

"Pull over," Mr. Jarvis said. "This is my lucky day." He got out and waited for the officer.

Seth sat, numb, straining to hear the conversation outside the car, catching only "father," "a real shame," "clueless" and "totally inept," a phrase that impressed Seth, considering that it issued from Mr. Jarvis. The chorus remained still, listening intently.

The officer approached the car and pointed to Seth. "You. At the courthouse. Saturday morning. Nine a.m."

Seth asked his mother to drop him off at the library, telling her he'd call when he was done, then walked the three blocks over to the courthouse. He had no idea what was going to happen, but he was determined to take his punishment like a man.

He found Officer Paul Goshen sitting in his police cruiser, eating a sausage-and-egg biscuit from Dairy Queen. "Punctual," he said. "Hop in."

Confused, Seth pointed to the courthouse. "Aren't we going in there?"

"What for?" asked Officer Goshen, a tall, young guy who looked like he had the potential to be friendly if he smiled. Not smiling, he pointed with a free thumb to the passenger seat. "No time for chin wagging."

Seth remained mystified when Officer Goshen pulled up in front of the Hope County regional police training academy. "It looks like it's closed," Seth ventured.

Officer Goshen jumped out of the car and opened a garage bay. "Help me with these cones."

Seth obeyed, dragging orange cones and arranging them on the parking lot at Officer Goshen's direction. Maybe the officer was cutting him a break and letting him do community service.

"All right, let's go." Seth dutifully trailed back to the police car and buckled himself into the passenger seat.

"Now pay attention." Officer Goshen stomped on the accelerator and the cruiser hurtled forward. He neatly negotiated one orange cone after another, chatting amicably the entire time. "Look where you want to go. Don't stare at the obstacle you're trying to dodge, because you'll drive right into it." The car darted in and out of the cones. "Maintain your throttle position and you'll maintain the car's balance."

"You mean keep your foot on the gas?" Seth asked.

"More or less. Now, let's say the weather's turned rotten and you're headed into a slide." Officer Goshen goosed the car into obliging and Seth felt his stomach tighten. "No problem. Give it a little gas, steer in the direction of the skid and you'll be just fine. Note that the rear is swinging to the right." Seth's stomach was well aware of the swing. "Just turn in the direction of the slide." Amazingly, the car did indeed straighten.

"Do the opposite of your natural instinct. Don't jump off the gas and don't hit the brakes. Remember, maintain your throttle position." Officer Goshen brought the car around to the start of the course. "Learn to communicate with your car."

"You can't communicate with a car," Seth said, then immediately wished he'd kept his mouth shut. He was already in enough trouble.

"Sure you can," Officer Goshen said. "That steering wheel talks all the time. So does the rest of the car. You start listening and you'll know when you're losing traction." He unbuckled. "Your turn."

"Oh, no," Seth said. "I'll wreck your car."

"Not with a skilled professional such as myself by your side."

"I know I'll run over every one of those cones." He was not about to humiliate himself further. It was a hopeless cause, anyway.

"The cones don't care."

"Look, I don't even know why you're doing this." It wasn't like a failing grade would keep Seth off the football team.

"I remember having a hard time figuring things out after I lost my dad." Officer Goshen turned in his seat to face Seth. When his mom tried to discuss his dad, Seth would just leave the room. Having nowhere to go now, he stared at the windshield.

"Look a man in the eye when you're talking to him," Officer Goshen said in a tone that was not a request. Seth complied. "You've given a lot of effort to letting people tell you what you can't do. I believe you can spare one day to find out what you're capable of doing."

"But Mr. Jarvis says—"

"Razor Jarvis is an idiot." Officer Goshen grinned. "Though I'd just as soon you didn't quote me on that. Let's start with just following the course. You can practice pirouettes later."

Seth ran over every cone, again and again. "You're just getting warmed up. Repetition is the key to success," Officer Goshen said as they set up the course one more time. "You're actually doing me a favor. I was supposed to go outlet mall shopping with a member of the female persuasion. I figure if we stay out at least until two or three, I'll be off the hook altogether."

Eventually, Seth began negotiating the course with more skill, finally completing one circuit with all the cones still pointing heavenward. "Now add some speed," Officer Goshen said. "Try inducing a skid."

Seth could not bring himself to move the car forward. "I, I—"

"You're afraid," Officer Goshen said, calmly stating what Seth had tried to deny even to himself. The officer pointed to the chain of gray-limbed hills lining the horizon.

"Here's something handy I learned in martial arts. I think the instructor got it from some monk: Breathing in, I am a mountain." Officer Goshen paused in the unwrapping of a stick of gum to noisily fill his diaphragm. "Breathing out, I am solid. Try it."

No way was he going to embarrass himself. Seth sat in silence.

"Don't make me use my service revolver."

Probably, the officer was kidding, but Seth inhaled a mighty breath, focusing on the scene before him. He was a mountain. He exhaled with a sigh, feeling a settling in his stomach. He was solid.

Officer Goshen popped the gum, smelling of cinnamon, in his mouth. "Enough preaching. Let's do it."

Seth hesitated, forgetting he was a mountain and envisioning the cruiser plowing right into the academy building. "Don't worry about the car. If you lose control, I'll shove you out the door and take over."

Seth laughed. He hadn't laughed in a long time.

"Mr. Jarvis, you're not going to let him drive? In this weather?" The whining came from Nod in the back seat.

"He has to log his time, just like the rest of you." Mr. Jarvis peered at the snowflakes wafting onto the hood of the driver's ed car. "Besides, I think it's letting up."

Seth buckled up, started the car, turned on the headlights, checked the mirrors and began smoothly accelerating down the school driveway. He maneuvered the car onto the highway, heading for Mutt's Mini-Mart.

The snow was not letting up. It fell thicker and faster, the resounding pings against the windshield leading Seth to suspect the involvement of ice. Mr. Jarvis's cell phone rang. "You want me to pick up what? And what else? Am I going to have to make a list?" With his free hand, Mr. Jarvis began patting his jacket pockets for a pen.

The windshield wipers swished back and forth. Breathing in, Seth was a mountain. Breathing out, he was solid. He gave his signal, looked in the rearview mirror and eased into the left lane, anticipating the turn toward Mutt's. The pickup that had seemed a reasonable distance back came roaring up behind him, then cut over to the right lane to pass, the driver gesturing his displeasure.

His hands began to sweat. Don't focus on the other driver's behavior. Keep your mind on the road, Officer Goshen had told him. That, and tend to your own rat-killing. Breathing in, he was a mountain. Breathing out, he was solid.

Dutifully scanning ahead, Seth saw the pickup that had just blown by him plow into the back of the Volvo. The car behind the pickup fishtailed right into the truck. Watching the chain reaction, Seth gently lifted his foot from the gas pedal, trying to slow down gradually, but he felt the car lose traction, the rear starting to break loose. At Nod's scream, Mr. Jarvis looked up and cursed, his intent clearly aimed at jabbing the instructor's brake.

"Leave the brake alone," Seth ordered. Mr. Jarvis's moment of shock gave Seth time to gently reapply pressure to the accelerator. He turned the car just before it could connect to the pileup, crossing the grassy median. If he stopped, the ground just might be soft enough to mire the vehicle. Keeping his foot on the gas to maintain momentum, Seth calculated he could execute a U-maneuver before the arrival of oncoming traffic in the two moving lanes. He straightened the car and kept driving, heart pounding but hands and feet steady.

"Dude, that was awesome," Winken said.

"Totally," Blinken agreed.

"If I'd been driving, we wouldn't have slid in the first place," Nod said.

"You want me to stop so we can switch drivers?" Seth asked his teacher.

"Don't stop now!" Mr. Jarvis swallowed. "I mean, we'd better get back in case classes dismiss early."

"You could call and find out," Winken suggested.

Seth spared a quick glance beside him. His teacher's hands trembled as they fumbled for the cell phone. "I think we've all had enough excitement for one day," Mr. Jarvis said.

Breathing in, Seth was a mountain. Breathing out, he was solid.

Reaper Man

LizBeth rushed out of the house to confront the man opening the door of her car. "What the hell do you think you're doing?"

The man paused and turned to grin at her. "Good to see you, too," he said, his voice smooth as polished rosewood. His forefinger slid his sunglasses down the bridge of his nose, revealing pale blue eyes and nearly transparent eyebrows that lent him an angelic appearance. He redirected his appraising glance to the small figure behind her. "Who's that? Your pet monkey?"

Annie giggled, but LizBeth shushed her. "Go back in the house." She turned her attention back to this man with his crisp white shirt, dark trousers and shoes polished to perfection. The vanilla and musk of his cologne hovered in the air.

LizBeth stood in frozen embarrassment, seeing her life through his assessing eyes: the little frame dwelling, which needed painting; the yard, which needed mowing; and her own sloppy outfit of T-shirt and denim cutoffs. When they'd first met, she still thought she could be the next singing sensation in country music. Instead, she had become trapped as a worker drone and mother.

"I'm calling Paul," LizBeth said, though she had no intention of doing so. "Breaking and entering, I think they call it."

"Who is that pretty man?" Annie piped up.

"Annie, you get inside right now."

The man's angelic smile widened. "You mean your momma's never shown you a picture of me? Maybe a wedding picture?"

"Lucius, don't you—"

"I could have been your daddy."

Annie shook her head. "My daddy's an Awful Sir."

"*Officer*," LizBeth said. "Now get inside. He's just a repo man."

Annie disappeared, only to appear a minute later with her head poking out a window. "My daddy's going to get you, Reaper Man. Breaking and entering."

"No, ma'am," he answered in that voice that sounded like the slow drip of maple syrup. He held up a computer-coded key. "Not when the dealer provides one of these. Then it's called asset recovery."

Giggles sailed from the window. "You said 'ass.' "

"*Annie*." The small head disappeared.

"I'm still calling Paul," LizBeth said. "You're not allowed on private property."

"Actually, I am, a fact of which you'd be cognizant if you'd read any of the notices your creditor sent you. I'm just trying to do you a favor."

"*You're* doing *me* a favor?"

"Save you the embarrassment of coming out of Piggly Wiggly with an armful of groceries and no car."

"I like chocolate," Annie hollered from the window. "That's my favorite favor."

"*Annie*. Don't make me come in there." The little head disappeared again. LizBeth looked around and saw a dark sedan parked on the street, its engine idling. "Look, you tell your partner we just got behind, but we're catching up." She could not let him take the Eclipse. She and Paul had bought that beautiful gold metallic turbocharged two-door trophy before they'd ever imagined the need for a child safety seat.

"A sad situation," Lucius agreed. "Maybe I could help you out. Got anything to offer in trade?" The glasses and his glance slid downward from the necklace glittering at her throat, and he tucked the key into his pants pocket.

LizBeth found her hand closing protectively around her pendant, feeling the rounded mound of the lapis cabochon and the ridges of the grape leaves, fashioned from genuine Black Hills gold. She probably shouldn't have bought it, but wearing it made her feel like a person of distinction. "You are so vile," she said.

"Impressive vocabulary, for a nurse's aid." He offered her that cherub's smile she remembered so well, the smile that had promised to take her to Nashville. But she remembered even more vividly the way the brightness always faded to surliness, to harsh words and that one time, that final time, a smack that sent her sprawling.

"Shouldn't you be in jail?"

"Reduced sentence. The judge took into account my vision problems on account of my albinism—"

"You're no albino." She looked at his eyes, at the unnaturally large pupils. "What are you on, anyway?"

"Babe, I'm always on." He smiled at her again. "You know, I could demand a DNA test."

"That's ridiculous—"

Just then a patrol car pulled up and Annie appeared again at the window. "I called my daddy, and he's going to get you, Reaper Man."

Paul Goshen got out of the car and strode over to the intruder, his lope a gawky contrast to the relaxed posture of LizBeth's first husband. LizBeth eased herself into a crouch on the stoop. Now there'd really be hell to pay. She twisted the silver cuff around her wrist in a worrying repetitive circle. She probably shouldn't have bought it, either, but its sheen provided an antidote to the ugly anonymity of her life.

"The word 'trespassing' mean anything to you?" Officer Goshen asked.

"The phrase 'payment due date' mean anything to

you?" Lucius replied pleasantly. He plucked a paper from the breast pocket of his shirt and handed it to Paul.

Paul puzzled over the document, frowning and handing it back to Lucius. It occurred to LizBeth that now might be a good time to disappear from her husband's line of sight. But just as she stood and turned toward the door, Paul caught up to her.

"You care to explain what's going on?" His voice issued low and deep, but she could see a flush crawling up from his shirt collar.

"We just got behind, that's all."

"We? You pay the bills. What have you been doing with our paychecks?" The flush rose into his face.

"I've been paying bills, that's what. Electricity. Telephone. Insurance. Cable so you can watch football." The best defense is a good offense. "And in case you haven't noticed, we have a child to provide for."

Said child hollered from the window. "Daddy, Daddy, the Reaper Man is getting away!"

Lucius waved from the driver's seat of the Eclipse. "I'd love to stay and visit," he called, "but I can see you two are busy." The Eclipse backed out of the driveway and disappeared down the street, followed by the sedan.

LizBeth threw up her hands. "You just let him take our car."

"No," Paul said, his voice dropping even lower. "You let him take our car. You want to tell me what's really going on?"

"Mommy," Annie called. "Can I watch my Pretty Ponies show, or do we have to watch the Jewelry Hour?"

Comprehension cleared the confusion on Paul's face. "Go watch your show, honey." After Annie's head bobbed away from the window, he folded his hands across his chest, tucking his hands under his arms. He eyed the glittering metal. "I thought you told me that was discount jewelry."

Knowing she couldn't make him understand, she attacked instead. "Don't you stand there like Mr. Officer and judge me."

"What else am I supposed to do when obviously you've spent our car payments on that junk?"

"You didn't think it was junk when you told me how good I looked." Wanting to spit more venom, she instead found herself starting to cry. She sank back onto the stoop

"Don't do that."

"I can't help it." She tried to use her thumbs to stop the ruination of her mascara.

"Come on." Paul sighed and sat beside her, wrapping an arm around her. "You always look good. You don't need that stuff." He handed her a handkerchief.

She stopped crying long enough to wipe her nose and say, "I need *something*. Every day, I have to wear that hateful uniform. Every day, I go into Mrs. Moore's room to turn down her radio, and I get reminded I'll never hear my voice coming out of that box." Her lip quivered and she feared she'd start tearing up again. "I need something to make me feel like my own person."

Paul squeezed her shoulder. "You got Mr. Echols asking you all the time to elope with him. That ought to make you feel pretty good about yourself."

"Yeah, well, he can't even find his own dentures."

"Plus, you got a good-looking husband and a beautiful daughter." Just then the beautiful daughter emitted a wail that carried through the walls. LizBeth and Paul leapt to their feet and raced into the house to find Annie holding aloft a bleeding index finger.

"OK, OK, OK, I know you said no scissors, but—" she began, having learned offensive strategy from the best.

"Let's patch you up," LizBeth said, heading for the

first-aid box in the kitchen.

Paul carried Annie, settling her on his lap at the table. "Hand me one of those antiseptic wipes," he said to LizBeth.

"No," Annie said. "You don't know how to do it, Daddy. I want Mommy to do it."

LizBeth sat beside them and quickly wiped away the thin line of blood. "It hurts, Mommy!"

LizBeth kissed the wound three times. Gently, she smoothed a bandage over the cut. "Better?"

Annie nodded, crawling from Paul's lap into LizBeth's. "I'm sorry," she said, snuggling against LizBeth. "Can we start over?"

"Can we?" LizBeth asked, looking at Paul.

He looked back at her. "Can you live without cable?"

"Can you live without football?" Submissiveness just wasn't in her nature.

"Yeah, I reckon I can. But just cutting the cable won't dig us out of this hole." He considered her bracelet and diamond dial watch. "E-bay, here we come."

"You can't be serious." Without her jewelry, she had no armor against obscurity.

"Serious as sh—" Paul paused. "As the monkey that lost his bananas." Annie giggled.

"I'll give up my watch and bracelet if you'll give up that new Remington." LizBeth knew he'd never agree to such a sacrifice.

"Not my hunting rifle! You can't be serious."

"That gun cost more than everything I'm wearing." Sure that he'd back down now, she cuddled Annie close.

"Ow, Mommy, you're hurting me." Annie struggled to pull back, revealing the indentation of a grape leaf on her cheek.

"Let me see," LizBeth said, reaching to rub the

imprint from her child's soft skin, but Annie turned away, hiding her face.

LizBeth unhooked the clasp and dropped the necklace on the table, intending only to placate her daughter. But as Annie settled against her again, LizBeth hesitated, then removed the cool metal cuff and the diamond dial watch.

"Looks like we have a deal," Paul said, extending his arm across the table. His long fingers traced the tan line exposed by the absence of her watch. He scooped up the jewelry and deposited it in his pants pocket, grinning at her. "Just in case you have second thoughts."

Too late for second thoughts, too late to be the freshest young voice from the mountains. Yet she couldn't gaze at that lopsided smile and continue to wallow in regret. "Just make sure you don't forget the case when you auction the Remington." LizBeth stroked Annie's hair, dark as onyx, and felt the heat of her little girl's body pressed to her heart.

Strawberry Pie

"I wonder who Earl has today?" Wanda slowed her old Buick to creep past the funeral home. A man in a pickup swerved around her and raised an unfriendly finger. "That was rude."

"What?" asked Rosalind. She'd been rooting in her purse for her rouge, pausing briefly when she came across the audiologist's appointment card, dated for the day before.

"I said, I wonder who Earl has today," Wanda hollered at her cousin.

"Don't yell at me. I'm not deaf." Rosalind flipped the visor down to squint at the little rectangle of a mirror. She drew her mouth into an oval as she massaged color into the hollows of her cheeks.

Rosalind and Wanda didn't resemble each other much, except for their cloud-white hair. Rosalind's lay in gentle waves, soft as her round body. Wanda's hair looked like she'd cut it herself, in a hurry.

"Do you mean Earl Junior, or Earl the Third?"

"The third, of course. Earl Junior spends most of his time in Florida. Earl the Third doesn't know how to relax. jumpy. That's the word. Like he's expecting somebody to rear up out of a coffin and ask for a refund."

"Earl doesn't have anybody," Rosalind said with confidence.

"Well, there was a state police car parked there. He must have somebody." Wanda had forgotten to resume her speed, and a line of vehicles formed a procession behind her.

"He can't have anybody. I checked the paper."

Rosalind kept a scrapbook of obituary clippings, indexed by surname. Every morning, she brewed a cup of coffee, then set to work with her scissors.

"I know what I saw."

Rosalind knew Wanda considered her unreliable just because she was three years younger. She dug into her big black purse again, hunting for her grocery list. "Isn't it nice having a Father's Day picnic at the church?" Rosalind had never married. There was one boy, a long time ago, but then he'd enlisted and never answered her letters. She still thought at times about the feel of his lips on hers, but no longer knew whether her mind presented her memory or fantasy.

At first, she searched the newspaper's casualty listings, dreading the discovery that he'd fallen in Germany. Or maybe Normandy or Guam. She still searched, in the hope that one day his hometown newspaper would tell her that he had lived a long and productive life. It could never tell her what she really wanted to know, but perhaps she would learn whether he became an Elk or an Odd Fellow, whether he married and had children.

"What are you taking to the picnic?" Rosalind asked, grateful for Father's Day, because it balanced the pain of that day in May when other women received cards and phone calls and jewelry sparkling with family birthstones.

"I don't know. Butterscotch pie." Wanda had previously expressed irritation at the very idea of the church making the women put on a spread. In her opinion, the men ought to get off their sorry behinds and do something for their women. It wouldn't kill a man to wash a dish, but that time she was down with her back, Chester just filled the sink with dirty plates, cups, utensils and pans.

"Oh, no, I wanted to make a butterscotch pie."

Wanda pulled into the grocery parking lot,

straddling two spaces. "Make one if you want."

Rosalind, who wouldn't dream of competing with Wanda's fluffy meringue, considered Wanda's move from Princeton to Hope County a divine tribulation visited upon her. She stepped from the car, following her cousin into the store and directly to the produce aisle, wondering if she ought to just make a cobbler. She picked up a carton of dewy red strawberries. A fresh strawberry pie would really stand out.

"You're a richer woman than me if you can afford those strawberries," Wanda said. She grabbed a bunch of over-ripened bananas, smelling of sweet decay, but reduced in price. "Maybe I'll make banana pudding."

"What are you planning to wear Sunday?" Wanda slowed as she approached the funeral home, which showed no sign of Officer Goshen's cruiser. Just two hearses and Earl the Third's Jeep Cherokee.

"What?" Rosalind had been checking her grocery receipt, which included two cans of cherries for an economical cobbler.

"I said," Wanda repeated, this time at a thunderous level, "What are you wearing Sunday?"

"I don't know. Probably pants, since it's a picnic. And you don't have to yell."

"I'm going to wear my green dress. We are going to be at church." She pulled abruptly into Earl's parking lot, turning right in front of a truck, eliciting a curse yelled out a window.

Rosalind looked up at the distant sound of discord. She'd been doublechecking the cash register receipt. It wasn't that the clerk would cheat her on purpose, but those computer scanners did make mistakes. "What are you doing?"

"I know he's got someone in there." Wanda was out

of the car and hobbling to the door. Rosalind, deciding she'd better wear a dress to the picnic, followed Wanda into the mortuary, which smelled of lemony pine. They trod soundlessly, their footsteps swallowed by the plush carpeting.

Earl the Third hurried out of his office at the soft chime of the door opening. "Ladies, good to see you. How are you?"

"Who you got today?" Wanda asked. Even her sharp voice seemed softened, absorbed by the velvety burgundy chairs and love seats provided for the bereaved.

Earl fiddled with the knot of his dark tie, then said, "We don't have services scheduled today."

"That's not what I asked. Who you got back there?"

"I'm not sure."

Rosalind hadn't heard most of the exchange, but Earl looked to her like a rabbit trembling, trying not to move, hoping the predator will move on. "Wanda, that butter is going to melt. And the chicken might go bad."

But Wanda's eyes shined like newly minted pennies. "You don't even know who you've got?"

"No, ma'am." Earl tightened his tie.

"How is it that you don't know who you've got?"

"Seems he had a heart attack at the rest stop on the interstate."

"So what does his wallet say?"

"Seems someone took advantage of his situation." Earl shook his head at the sorry state of civilization. "His wallet was missing, and the stereo in his car, too."

"Well, let us take a look."

"Oh, I'm sure you wouldn't want to see—"

Wanda cut him off. "Maybe he was on his way to visit relatives here. Let us see."

There is no force as unstoppable as an old woman who has made up her mind. Earl sighed and said, "We've already prepared the body. I guess we can consider this a viewing." He led her down the hall, trailed by Rosalind, who had no idea where she was headed. Then she saw the casket.

"Who is it, Wanda?"

"We're about to find out." Wanda marched right up to the coffin. "Good-looking fellow, considering. I'd say he was in his seventies, but you don't find too many men that age with that much hair on their head."

Rosalind peeped around her cousin. It couldn't be. But despite the silver color of the hair, she instantly recognized that boy that left her so long ago. Wrinkles couldn't disguise those strong, handsome features. The world started to lift away from her, and she grabbed the edge of the casket.

Rosalind hadn't noticed the coffin rested on a wheeled support. As the apparatus began to slide, she found herself swinging in a circle with her dead lover. Shrieking in fear, she gripped even tighter. Before Earl or Wanda could move, the coffin slid to the floor, with Rosalind collapsed beside it, crying.

Earl rushed to help raise Rosalind, but she waved him off.

"Are you hurt?" Wanda yelled.

"No, I'm not hurt," Rosalind said. "My heart's broke, that's all."

"You'd better get up and make sure you're not hurt."

"Leave me alone." Rosalind cried some more and Earl quietly set a box of tissues beside her.

"She could be hurt," Wanda said to Earl. "We could sue."

Earl twitched and started to sweat. "Oh, now, I'm sure—"

"Get out." Rosalind fixed her rage on Wanda.

"You're hysterical," Wanda said, unmoving.

Rosalind, who had never even smashed a spider, threw the box of tissues, hitting Wanda in the arm. One sharp corner pricked the skin, drawing a bit of blood.

At Wanda's first howl, Earl leapt into action, ushering Wanda out of the room. "I've got a first-aid kit, we'll get you all fixed up. How about some coffee? I've got decaf." His nervous chatter faded down the hall, leaving Rosalind alone with her lost love.

She couldn't remember his name. Every morning, she had searched for him, but now she couldn't summon his identity. She knew those lips, though. No longer so full and soft, but still inviting. Rosalind wiped her face with her hands and stared at the lover who promised so much and left her with nothing. She reached into the coffin for his left hand. No ring. It could have been stolen, but she didn't see an imprint of a band. Gently, she replaced the hand. The coolness of it felt almost pleasant.

Rosalind considered that dear face, gentle even in death, and began to supply her own answers. He was returning for her. Rosalind was more sure of his love than she had ever been of anything in her life. She leaned into the coffin and pressed her lips against those of the dead man, feeling nothing but the warmth of those kisses from so long ago.

In the office, Rosalind found Wanda wearing a bandage and haranguing Earl. "Wanda, I'm going back to the store."

"Can't it wait until later?" Wanda picked at the adhesive covering her injury. "My arm hurts."

"If you're just going to sit there, give me the keys and I'll drive myself." Rosalind hadn't heard so much for so long, but now she caught the authority in her own voice.

Wanda stood obediently. "I'm ready to go. Just what is it you need so bad?"

"I *want* some strawberries," Rosalind said. "I'm going to make a strawberry pie. I might just make a butterscotch, too."

Unplugged

"Go ahead and pull the plug," a woman's voice says. *Please. Be my guest.* That sorry excuse for an air conditioner roars constantly, tickling my skin, but I can't scratch. I'm stuck in a bed that Hope County General Hospital must have installed thirty years ago, unable to move or see or talk. I can feel, though. I spend hours feeling a wrinkle in the sheet rubbing my backside raw.

"Don't tempt me," a man's voice answers. A doctor? An orderly? "I can't believe you were married to that low life." Wait a minute. That drawl sounds familiar.

"What can I say? I was eighteen, and he had a Trans Am." The woman's voice is that of LizBeth, my ex-wife who filed divorce papers almost before the prison door could slam shut on me. The guy must be Officer Paul Goshen, LizBeth's current husband and my second DUI ticket.

I have to feel sorry for LizBeth, chained to a clown, working as a nurse's aide to feed their rug rat. She should have stuck by me. A talented recovery specialist can make a good living, and I am a talented guy. My old man died in a coal mine and my momma drowned her sorrows in cough syrup, so I am naturally immune to hard-luck stories. Pay up or give it up, I say. When the deadbeats switch to repo men insults, I just tap in the key code that the car dealer gave me and make the pop.

"What you're asking me to do is illegal," Goofy Goshen says. "Besides, he might still come out of it. You never know about comas."

"I know plenty," LizBeth says without a speck of sorrow. "I've seen plenty. They shrivel, and they finally die.

157

What's the point?"

Cold starts creeping over me, and it's got nothing to do with the air conditioning unit. Suddenly, I remember the time when that tree got in the way of my Trans Am and before I went into surgery I signed a form, a medical power of attorney or something like that. *Hey, that doesn't give you the right—*

"The point is that the doctors think he could still come out of it. Where you work, all you see are old people." A wrapper crinkles, someone begins chomping, and the fresh aroma of cinnamon gum floats through the room.

"Suffering is suffering." I don't hear compassion, but I do smell the jasmine of her cologne as she nears me. Her sweet scent envelopes me, and I remember the good times. Maybe I could have held my temper better. But she should have known not to provoke me. I'd learned that lesson myself as a kid.

Suddenly, I feel my pillow sliding away. *Don't let her smother me*, I scream at the current husband. *It's murder.* But it's not murder. Instead, she moves the pillow to cradle my neck and I have to admit I feel more comfortable.

"You want me to pull the plug, but you're adjusting his pillow," Goshen observes.

"Force of habit," LizBeth says, and the sweet cloud of scent withdraws. "I hate to see even a poor dumb animal suffering."

"You don't know that he's suffering."

That's right, I want to shout. *That's right. You don't know that I'm suffering.*

"Let's find out. This little piggy went to market." Suddenly, I feel the rush of air over my uncovered foot and a tugging on my big toe. "This little piggy came home wasted. This little piggy broke all his promises. This little piggy waved a gun. And this little piggy—" I feel a wrenching pain in my little toe. "See, not a twitch or a blink."

"I can't believe you did that." The gum snaps faster, as though the chewer is getting nervous.

"So are you going to help me or not?" A hacksaw couldn't cut through the metal of LizBeth's voice. Yet she's tucking the sheet back over my feet like she's afraid I'll catch pneumonia.

Just say no.

"Look, I know he treated you bad, Dor—" He stops, but Tropical Storm LizBeth lashes out.

"Did you just call me by your old girlfriend's name?"

There's a choking sound that might be the accidental swallowing of gum. "No, no, I was saying, darlin'—"

"I'm out of here," LizBeth says. "I'm taking that paper straight to the hospital administrator." She whips out of the room, the air whooshing from the door to sweep over my bed. The antiseptic smell of the hallway mixes with the musty odor from the air conditioner. I hear Goshen's feet shuffle, as though he's undecided whether to stay or go.

If I could, I'd laugh. LizBeth can wave that paper all she wants, but there's no way the hospital lawyers will allow an ex-wife to terminate with extreme prejudice. I'm going to skate out of this scrape just like I skated out of prison. I could have gotten three years for that third DUI, but I talked the judge into the minimum of one year, and no fine. I've been thinking a lot about my current situation and how I'm going to explain to the judge just why I was driving on a revoked license and how I wound up wrapped around a telephone pole with a bottle by my side. Luckily for me, that was all they found.

Before I can contemplate further about how I might

work the remorse angle, the reek of Pine Sol — correction, Officer Goshen's aftershave — drifts over my bed. "I can't think of a guy who deserves it more," he mutters.

Don't even think about it, you— Then I feel a shifting in my body, like an earthquake fault cracking open. Pain rips from my neck to my spine, streaking down my legs. I try to concentrate on my breathing, waiting for the torment to pass.

Instead, it circles back and makes another run, grabbing hold of my neck and then sledding down my spinal cord, this time coasting all the way to my feet. If only I could scream. Here it comes again, stinging every nerve like a sheet of sleet.

I try to pray. *Give me a break*, I say to whatever higher authority might be on call. Just as I'm trying to decide whether to offer to give up drinking, the demon pain comes knocking again, this time with a torch.

I can't take this. No human could. I can't spend months or years of such torture. I can't take even one more minute. *Please*, I beg Goshen. *Unplug me.*

I sense him leaning over me, then drawing back. "I can't do it."

Unplug me, I demand. *Unplug me*, I plead with him. *Release me*, I pray to the Great Warden in the Sky.

Then, a miracle. The little toe on my right foot, the one LizBeth pinched, twitches. At first, I dismiss it as a phantom memory of movement. Still, my fried brain sends an experimental signal. The toe moves.

Open, sesame, I command my eyes. The lids strain as though they're weighted by anchors, but they lift. At first, I see only patterns of light and shadow. Then, the shape of Goshen materializes. Prison couldn't hold me, and neither can this coma. I'll tell the judge about how I saw the light and how smacking that telephone pole made me a different man.

Get a doctor. I command myself to speak. *Get a doctor.* My jaw creaks open, emitting nothing intelligible. But it's the start of sound, no mistake about it.

My vision, growing sharper, locks on Goshen gaping at me like a little boy who just saw Santa sliding down the chimney. "Well, I'll be—" He whirls around, hollering LizBeth's name. He bolts for the door. Or tries to, but his snowshoe feet tangle themselves in the cords of the life support equipment.

I can't see the plug being yanked from the socket, but I feel the sudden draining of my resurrection. Careful what you pray for, the prison chaplain once cautioned me. *No,* I protest. *Wait. No—*

Blackness replaces my eyesight. There's a roaring in my ears and the feeling that I'm being sucked into a tunnel. Dimly, as though I'm standing on the other side of a river from myself, I hear the sound of someone gasping for air like a trout flopping on the bank. Just barely, I catch the scent of jasmine.

"I can't believe you actually did it." I can hear LizBeth tinkering with the equipment, but she sounds far away. I'm sliding down the rabbit hole.

Then, suddenly, I can breathe again. Must be back online. I knew it. *You still love me. You'll always love me.*

"Paul." I remember that husky warm womanly tone, but the name is wrong. "You did that for me. I was coming back to tell you that I couldn't—"

"Actually, I didn't mean—"

"I can't believe you risked your job like that, for me."

"To tell the truth—" The talking stops and I hear the disgusting sounds of the two of them kissing.

Hey, what about me? The darkness begins to fade. Maybe I'm getting my vision back. Something's not right, though. My eyes won't open, but I'm surrounded by neon white light. The light grows, washing over me the way snow can make the highway disappear. Instinct tells me to fight, but the light is too strong.

Come on, I've made it this far. Give me a break—

Appraisal

The woman stands at the bank of the stream, her hands cradling her swollen belly. The water shimmers in the September sun, inviting her in, but she hesitates. Even though the water looks to be only ankle deep, she knows treachery awaits if she crosses the creek bed of slick rock.

But she has no other choice. Behind her lies the slaughter of her menfolk. She picks up her little cotton knapsack, comforted by the weight of a small silver cream jug. Foolish to continue to carry it when she's lost everything of true value. As foolish as her father and husband in their confidence they could claim a homeland for themselves by clearing a patch of wilderness. Yet she cannot surrender this one last reminder of civilization.

1777. The country has declared itself independent, but the woman has yet to find freedom – from want, from sorrow, from danger. She frowns at the creek and steps forward. There is nothing for it but to cross.

"You're kidding." Margaret gawked open-mouthed at the "Antiques Appraisal Hour" camera, though she knew she was supposed to be looking at the lady from Sotheby's.

"No, indeed," the appraiser said, her voice as smooth and cool as the silver jug that sat between them on a display table in the civic center.

"You're joking," Margaret said. She knew the creamer was old, handed down from Virginia settler to West Virginia great-grandmother. Maybe even worth a few hundred dollars.

"Absolutely not." The appraiser, who smelled like an expensive blend of sandalwood and real vanilla, pointed a well-manicured finger at the primitive birds etched on the shiny surface. Margaret's hands could look like that, if she didn't have to scrub pots and pans. "This is just so rare in an 18th-century American piece."

Margaret always had thought the birds primitive, an amateur's attempt at art. "You're just yanking my chain." The frown that briefly flashed on the appraiser's face told Margaret this was not the kind of phrase used on a public television show.

"Absolutely not," the woman repeated. "This would easily bring $50,000 to $60,000 at auction."

"It's got quite a story behind it," Margaret began, unable to comprehend such a sum. "See, Mary Bird was my great-grandmother, several times removed, of course—"

"Thank you so much for coming today." The appraiser and cameraman turned to the next hopeful face, and Margaret found herself being led away by her husband.

"You want to get something to eat?" Ed asked. They were standing on the sidewalk outside the civic center. In one hand she clutched a plastic grocery bag containing the jug, wrapped in a faded yellow dish towel. With the other, she shaded her eyes against the glare of the summer sun.

Ed said, "It'll take a crow bar to pry those boys away from the music store, but I bet if I mention Cracker Barrel—"

"How can you even think of eating?"

"Got to eat some time." He was a regular Jack Sprat. Margaret suspected that she gained weight on the fumes from his food.

"Are you crazy? We can't go anywhere in public." Margaret clutched the bag more tightly. "We can't even go home. Someone will knock us in the head and steal the jug."

"Who's going to know what you might be carrying

in that sack?"

"Anyone with a television set."

Ed hooted. "Did you think that was broadcast live, like the Final Four?"

"Oh." Of course. "Still, there were people all around us."

Ed gazed around him. "I don't see a thing but those sorry-looking pigeons." A couple of birds that had been scuffling over a discarded hamburger bun paused, glared at the couple, and returned to their bickering.

"We'd better go straight to the bank and store it in a safety deposit box." Traffic streamed by, drenching the humid air with gasoline fumes.

"This is Saturday, sugarpie."

They continued to argue about the disposition of the jug as they walked over to the mall, where they found Eddie and Jimmy in the music store, glued to listening posts, sampling track after track. As Ed predicted, only the promise of Cracker Barrel could lure them away.

"Can we get these, Dad?" Eddie asked, holding out a handful of CDs. Margaret flashed back briefly to an image of elementary-school Eddie begging for a Barney videotape.

"Why not?" Ed answered jovially. "Seeing as how—"

"Ed Riner, we are not going to start spending money we don't even have yet."

Jimmy's ears, which were showing signs of becoming just as prominent as Ed's, flapped to full reception. "Yet? What money?" He eyed the bag. "That old jug, is it worth a lot?" He started to execute a touchdown victory dance. "We're rich!"

"Hush." Margaret hugged the bag to her chest. "And no Cracker Barrel if you can't keep your mouths shut." She was starting to wish she'd never agreed to Ed's suggestion to have the jug appraised. His years of selling NASCAR collectibles compelled him to constantly calculate the worth of objects.

Margaret didn't need some outsider to tell her the creamer's value. The tale of Mary Bird had been handed down through generations of mountain women. Tough as spruces, they'd each cherished the small chunk of metal that had been fashioned into something fine. One hand crept to her chest, to touch the heart-shaped charm with three birthstones, remembering with sorrow that the story ended with her.

Paul Goshen stood at the shore of a shallow spot along the New River, wondering how something at least a few million years old could be called new. He'd read somewhere that Thomas Jefferson's father, out surveying, named it so simply because it was new to him. Better, he supposed, than River of Death, a nickname the Cherokees formulated after some of their relatives found out the hard way about the mean currents further along the stream.

But it was time now to impart his philosophy of fishing to his progeny. Allow the prey to offer itself. Patience reaps rewards. Stillness leads to victory. The day could not be finer for fishing — overcast, warm but with a little breeze. The air smelled fresh, charged with the energy of the river. He tugged at the back of his lucky red baseball cap with one hand and pulled at the brim with the other to position it for maximum effectiveness.

His daughter squatted beside the ice cooler, flipping back the lid and withdrawing an old margarine tub filled with worms. "I'm ready, Daddy."

"OK, honey, hand me a worm and I'll hook him for you."

"I want to do it," Annie said in protest.

"That hook's sharp. Better let me do it." Watching

the disappointment and stubbornness clouding her face, he added, "But you pick the worm that's got the best chance of catching us a fish."

Annie shook the container and peered at its contents. Solemnly, she selected a worthy specimen and handed it to Paul. He took it from her gravely and hooked the worm three times to secure it.

"Daddy, you're killing it!" Annie screamed at the sight of the wiggling ends and began to cry.

Paul froze, paralyzed. This was not how his first fishing trip had gone with his father. Finally, he said, "Honey, think about all those hungry fish. They need something to eat, too." Quickly, he cast, sending the hook and bobber into the water. He handed the pole to Annie.

Five minutes later, Annie said, "Can we go now?"

"Go? You've been begging me all summer to take you fishing." Paul remembered how eagerly he had looked forward to spending a whole day with his father.

"My arm's tired."

Paul took the pole from her. "I'll hold it for you until your fish comes calling."

Annie seated herself on the cooler. "Daddy?"

"What?"

"When you sell my toys, can I keep one doll?"

"Why would I sell your toys?"

"To pay the reaper man."

"The reaper man?"

"You know, the one that wanted your car?"

"Oh. Don't you worry, honey. He won't be coming back." Paul scanned the water's surface. "I wish I had that lantern that Diogenes carried around."

Annie, who had started drawing in the dirt with a stick, said, "Is this a story?"

"No, it's history." Or at least it was to the best of his recollection of his time at the community college.

"Diogenes went around in the daytime with a lantern, looking for an honest man." He did not mention that Diogenes also had the odd notion that living in a tub was a suitable habitat for a philosopher.

"What's a lantern?"

"I guess you could say it's a sort of lamp."

"Oh, like Aladdin's lamp."

"No, not exactly." Paul searched the surface of the water for any sign of movement. "More like a flashlight in a box."

"You have to use a flashlight at night, Daddy," Annie said.

"That's what made it special. That's what I need to find us a fish."

"How come he went looking in the daylight with his lantern? That don't make sense."

"No," Paul said, looking without hope upon the still water. "I don't reckon it does."

Margaret and her men had gone to the Cracker Barrel, where the boys had tormented her until she'd revealed the appraiser's estimate.

"We can get a new game system," Jimmy said. "And a flat-screen TV."

"I want an MP3 player," Eddie said.

"Fellas, you're thinking small time," Ed said, biscuit in one hand, fork in the other, using them to dredge every last bit of meat loaf and mashed potatoes.

"What do you have in mind, Dad?" Eddie, now in seventh grade, was talking man to man.

The biscuit disappeared with the meat and potatoes. "Bass boat."

Mount Margaret erupted. "First," she said, pointing her fork at Ed, "We don't have the money. Second, if we do get the money, we're going to invest it and save it for college. This is the only inheritance we'll ever have."

"You can go ahead and let me have my share." Eddie prepared to bite another chunk from his hamburger. "I'm not going to need college for my career."

"Oh?" Margaret asked. "And what career would that be?"

"Asset recovery specialist."

"A what?" Margaret stopped toying with her cod fillet.

"You know, a repo man. Like the movie."

"I want my share right now, too," Jimmy announced. "I'm not going to college, either."

"But you told me you wanted to be an archaeologist."

"That was a long time ago," he said, though in fact he had just talked about it the day before. "I'm going to be a repo man, too."

In the minivan on the way home, Margaret sat with the bag in her lap, feeling the burden of the jug. She stared out the window at the landscape, watching the cityscape of gray boxy buildings yielding to rolling hills thick with the green of summer. She considered rolling down the window to sniff for honeysuckle, then dismissed the notion as foolishness.

"Mom, can I look at it?" one of the boys called from the back seat of the van.

"You've seen it," Margaret said.

"But I want to hold it," Jimmy said.

"You don't need to hold it."

"Please." Then the little devil added, "After all, it is *my* inheritance."

"*And* mine," Eddie said.

"Not if you die first," Jimmy said. "Like Aimee."

Margaret felt her heart constrict at the mention of the name that never had a chance to grow into a person.

"Oh, great," Eddie muttered. "Now you've done it."

Before she could speak, Margaret found herself suddenly pitching forward, the bag sliding from her grip. Ed braked and cursed as a doe bounded across the highway and into the woods beyond the shoulder of the road.

"Ed, slow down." The seat belt had ratcheted to catch her and pin her against the seat, and she struggled to reclaim the bag. "This is not a Corvette. Slow down," she repeated as the minivan approached the New River Gorge Bridge. "Bridges make me nervous."

Ed lifted. "Fellas, it's not likely you'll cross a bridge higher than this one. Used to be the longest steel-arch bridge in the world, too, until the Chinese got busy."

"Hey, is this where they bungee jump?" Eddie asked. "You know, when they have that festival?"

"What's bungee jump?" Jimmy wanted to know.

"You tie a rope around your waist, attach the other end to the bridge, then you jump off the bridge and the rope bounces you like a Yo-Yo."

"Cool – I want to do that. Can we come back and do that? Can we?"

"It's called base jumping, and you use a parachute, not—" Ed began. "Uh oh. That can't be good."

"What?" Margaret's tenseness in crossing the bridge contracted into a tight knot.

"There's blue smoke coming out the back," Eddie informed the occupants of the front seat.

"What's that sound? Pull over."

"We're all right," Ed said, but Margaret saw how tightly he gripped the steering wheel. As soon as they cleared the bridge, Ed stopped the minivan on the side of the road. The boys jumped out, exclaiming in admiration. Margaret unbuckled and headed for the boys, but her scolding about watching for traffic was halted by the sight of the nearly bare wheel. Rubber shreds, spewed along the shoulder, lay like slaughtered snakes in a line that stretched beyond her vision.

"Blowout," Jimmy said, impressed.

"I didn't feel anything," she said.

Ed pointed at the radial belt still valiantly clinging to the wheel. "Modern technology." He headed toward the back of the vehicle. "Wonder where that jack is?"

Eddie followed his father, but Jimmy took the opportunity to slip inside the front passenger door and grab the grocery bag. "What are you doing?" Margaret asked, but Jimmy already had the creamer in his hands.

"I'm just looking."

"You've looked. Put it back."

"Hey, what's going on?" Eddie strode to his brother, reaching for the jug. "Let me see. I never held $50,000."

Jimmy resisted. "Let go."

"You let go, squirt."

"Quit it, you two." Margaret started to reach for the creamer herself just as Eddie wrested it from his younger brother's grasp. Six hands danced in the air, jostling the jug — and sending it plummeting nearly a thousand feet to the canyon's bottom.

The silence caught Ed's attention and he appeared from behind the minivan. "What's going on?" he asked, jack in hand.

"Jimmy threw Mom's jug in the river," Eddie said.

"It was your fault," Jimmy protested. "Dad—"

"Give it a rest," Ed commanded.

"We've got to go get it," Margaret said, starting to walk down the shoulder of the highway, her tear-filled eyes darting to find a bank where she could clamber down to the river.

"Sugarpie, it's gone. You'll break your neck if you try going down there." Ed trapped her in his arms at the edge of a steep slope covered with trees and brambles. "Besides, the place is covered up in poison oak."

"No, we have to find it." She thought of her ancestor, Mary Bird, and began to seriously cry.

"The river's got it now. Hard to tell where it could end up." Ed gave her a squeeze. "Easy come, easy go."

But its possession had never been easy. Margaret thought first of Mary Bird's pioneer struggles, and then of the ancestor who'd written in a letter to a cousin about how she'd managed to conceal the jug – and one chicken – from a marauding patrol during the War Between the States. She thought of her mother's mother, who'd confided that she'd hidden the creamer from her own husband back during the Depression. Margaret wondered if she should have done the same. Ed could and would sell anything.

Even his championship ring. Margaret fingered the heart on her necklace, rubbing the third stone, thinking of the grave marker that everyone told her she didn't need, to just forget and have more babies. Everyone but Ed, who'd sold the tribute to his baseball prowess to buy that little lamb-topped marble monument.

Margaret stared at the rushing water that had consumed the one tangible link to her heritage. She had thought the story would end with her, but perhaps Mary Bird had reclaimed the creamer for its intended.

"I'm sorry, Mom," Eddie said.

"I'm sorrier," Jimmy announced.

Margaret looked upon their penitent faces. With enough prodding, they might become decent men. Standing before her, still waiting to be shaped, was her legacy.

"Can I still have a Play Station?" Jimmy asked.

Can donkeys fly? She swallowed the sarcasm and instead began to forge the metal. "Can you make straight As this year?" Margaret asked. "You answer me that next June, and I'll answer your question."

Paul could tell by the tug that this was going to be a keeper. Whether it would be supper or trophy remained to be seen. Annie danced around him. "Watch it, Daddy. He'll get away."

Just then a silver missile came hurtling through the air and landed with a splash in the water. In surprise, Paul relaxed his grip on the pole, giving his prey the chance to escape.

While Paul stood gaping at the old jug that had fallen from the sky, Annie ran from the bank and into the water, wading past him to grab for the heaven-sent gift. "Come back here," he ordered, reaching for her. "Those rocks are slick."

She ignored him, as did most of the women in his life, eluding his grasp, already up to her knees in water as she pursued the twinkling treasure headed downstream. Paul plowed in after her, nearly slipping himself. Just as Annie latched onto the jug, waist deep, she lost her footing, giving a little gasp, but her father snatched her from the greedy river.

Back on shore, Annie examined her prize. "Daddy, Daddy, it's a magic lantern, like genies come in. Only—" She poured out the river water. "It's supposed to have a lid. Does that mean the genie's gone?"

"Honey, I don't think that's a lantern."

"Maybe it's Doggoknee's lantern."

"Who?"

"Doggoknees." Annie, her shorts sagging with river water, hugged her catch. "I'm going to keep it forever and ever." Then a frown crossed her face and she held out the catch. "No, you take it, Daddy."

"Why do you want me to have it?"

"Maybe you can sell it and then Mommy can keep her jewelry and I can keep my dolls."

Paul's heart squeezed in guilt. She'd tried to tell him before, but he hadn't heard, hadn't understood that all this time, his daughter had been grieving, willing to sacrifice her most beloved possessions. "You let me and Mommy worry about the bills. We're doing all right."

"Really truly?"

"Really truly." Paul removed his cap and held it to his chest, as though he were about to sing the national anthem. "Cross my heart and hope to fry."

Annie clasped the jug tight. "You know what I'm going to keep in it?"

"Dog biscuits?"

"No, Daddy."

"Jelly beans?"

"No."

What, then?"

"I'm not going to tell." Annie said. "It's always going to be my secret."

The woman weeps with rage and fear. She has come so far, borne her daughter by herself like a wild animal, walking, walking. The fort awaits just across the river, but the recent flooding makes fording out of the question. Yet her pursuers cannot be far behind. She shucks a petticoat and wraps her baby, securing little Mary Bird close to her heart. The knapsack, still heavy with the little cream jug, is tied at her waist.

Impossible to swim across a flooded river, but she wades into the stream, then hesitates, shocked by the force of the water. Knowing she can't turn back, she plunges into the water and begins to swim. She's halfway across the river when the petticoat ruptures, sending Mary Bird swirling away from her. She fights the current with desperation, reaching, reaching for the little body bobbing just out of her grasp.

With one final lunge, powered by a mother's love, she grabs the baby and fights her way to the shore. She lies panting on the ground, unable to move forward even one inch. Then Mary Bird coughs and cries, and the woman knows she has to push on to the fort, to warm and dry her baby. As she struggles to her feet, she sees half-clad figures emerging from the forest on the other side of the river. The creamer banging against her hip, she hastens toward the fort. She still hasn't found freedom, but she's arrived at sanctuary.

Remember Your Humanity

"What's your hurry?" I eyeballed the old man behind the wheel of the dark green Jaguar XJ12.

"I'm sorry, Officer," said the fellow. He wore some kind of Johnny Cash, legend-of-country music getup — black jacket and black pants. Standing slightly back of the driver's door, I could see tooled Western boots shining from the floorboard. He looked pretty sharp for an old dude, especially with that thick white hair flowing to his collar.

Johnny would have dressed all in black, though. This guy wore a white shirt and a bolo tie. On the seat beside him sat a magnificent Western Stetson. I wore a Stetson myself, though it was a campaign hat that made me look like Smokey Bear. Still, it covered my early indication of male pattern baldness. "You a gospel singer, by any chance?"

The old dude smiled, creating more creases in a face that had been broiled by the sun, or too many tanning bed sessions. "No, but I do enjoy a song of praise."

"Are you aware of the town's speed limit?" The answer, of course, would be no, but I felt compelled to complete this law enforcement ritual, even though I really didn't want to produce that hateful ticket book that requires an advanced degree in form filing. I'd already had two cases thrown out because I hadn't written the citations correctly.

It's not just the aggravation that makes me resist writing tickets. I got into law enforcement to help people, to be the kind of man my dad was. He believed in second chances. The chief, however, favors swift and non-appealable damnation.

"I'm fairly sure the sign said 25 miles per hour."

Unbelievable. A pure, unvarnished confession. Just then a UPS truck passed by, its tail wind sweeping my hat from my head. I jogged down the shoulder and captured my $120 Stetson just inches from a muddy pothole. If anything happened to that hat, the chief would first take the price out of my hide, and then my paycheck. I couldn't afford any deductions, not with the LesleyJo Rumpelstiltskin Series already on layaway. Sure, I could afford the $20 LesleyJo-as-the-miller's-daughter doll, but of course no little girl would want LesleyJo without the king doll, the dwarf doll, the spinning wheel and the plastic play castle.

When I returned to my prey, I jammed the hat back in place, tilting the brim toward my brow so I looked more like a Marine drill instructor, instead of the fire prevention bear. "And do you know how fast you were going?" He would, of course, deny all knowledge of breaking the limit. Maybe I could just give the old guy a warning.

"I'd say at least fifty miles an hour."

Never in my law enforcement career had anyone actually admitted to speeding. I couldn't see any way out of writing a ticket now. "You know I could haul you in for reckless endangerment."

"I've been accused of that before," the confessed criminal said agreeably.

Before I could ask the old coot whether he'd asked the nice doctor to borrow the car before he sneaked out of the institution, a coal truck roared by. My Stetson took flight, spinning in the air like a drunken blue jay, heading straight for an embankment covered with viney briers.

"No, no, no!" I screamed and took off. But I was too late. The wool felt attached itself to a thatch of briers, and just out of reach. No way could I climb that incline, steep and still slick from a recent downpour. I slipped my collapsible baton from my holster. If I wedged the club underneath, maybe I could flip the hat back to me, just like a game of Pick-up Sticks.

Measure twice, cut once, my dad used to say. I never found out exactly what he meant, because I was still pretty young when he died from the cancer he got after being exposed to some chemical overseas. It didn't occur to me that his advice might apply to this situation until I had slung the telescoping baton open in such a hurry that it leapt right from my hand, soaring over the guard rail and into one of those endless ravines that we West Virginians fondly call hollows.

"Well, pluck a little duck." Once, I would have elaborated with considerably more force, but living with a pre-schooler had changed the tenor of my oaths.

A debate over the advisability of plunging into the mud and brush after the baton was playing in my head when I heard the big-kitty rumble of a Jaguar engine starting. I turned around just in time to see the car streaking by, the old man waving like he'd enjoyed stopping to jaw with me, but now he had to be getting on home.

Running back to the cruiser, I took off in hot pursuit. I should have called for backup, but I didn't want to admit I hadn't got around to noting the license plate number. Incredibly, on a straight stretch, I caught sight of him topping a hill. I goosed the V-8. He was going to be one sorry senior when I hauled him out of that car.

No sign of the Jag, though, when I crested the hill. By this time, I was well out of town, in countryside heaving with green. Then I saw the old woman, sagging in the heat, struggling along on the shoulder of the road.

I braked hard and pulled over. There weren't any houses anywhere near here. She was dressed way too warm for the day, wearing an old-lady sweater over what looked like a Sunday church dress. She wore sneakers, but no socks, and clutched a huge white pocketbook. Right away, I figured she wasn't right in the head. It's true that I found my wife on the side of the road, too, but no way would LizBeth wear tennis shoes with a dress.

"Oh, thank goodness," the woman chirped as soon as I got out of the cruiser, hatless. "I had despaired of finding a cab in this desolate land, and was just about to take this shortcut." She was pointing to a dense patch of forest that could swallow sunshine and never even leave a shadow.

"Ma'am, I'm Officer Paul Goshen."

"In my day, you were called cabbies, but I suppose if a conductor is both a man who sorts musicians and a man who sorts passengers, then you can be an officer." She sidled right into the front passenger seat of my car. Before I could toss the Dairy Queen bag into the back seat, she had discovered the Blizzard and gulped the melted contents. "I was so thirsty," she said.

I slid into the driver's seat, resigned to having lost the Jaguar. This was going to take some time. I turned over the engine to get the air conditioner going. "Ma'am, if you tell me where you live, I'll take you home."

"Ah, now there's an interesting question," she said. "Let's see if we can find a clue in here." She opened the handbag and began passing me the contents, piece by piece: a handkerchief, a hairbrush and a half-eaten raisin cream cake, neatly saved in its original cellophane. She looked longingly at the cake before handing it over. "I'm famished, but I'd better save it for later." I got a little concerned when she took out a foot-long knitting needle with a mean-looking point, but she handed it over as though it was as common a purse item as a comb.

Not one scrap of paper. "Ma'am, what's your name?"

Tears trembled in her eyes, big blue eyes that

reminded me of an old girlfriend. I bet those eyes had hypnotized more than one boy. "You know, this is how it starts."

"How what starts?"

"I still know enough to understand that I should know my own name, and to be distressed that I don't." The tears trickled down the pouches of a worried face that still bore traces of a pert and determined woman. "Soon I won't even be able to utter a coherent sentence." She plucked the handkerchief from my hand and wiped at her face. "It's very trying, living at the edge of the abyss."

She stuffed the handkerchief back in her purse and began retrieving her other belongings from my hands. "There was a time when I wouldn't have dreamed of leaving the house without a compact and lipstick." She looked at me. "How can I know that and not know my name?"

"Let me call and see if anyone has reported you missing. I bet you've got family looking for you." I called the dispatcher from the car radio. She said she didn't have any missing persons reports, but she'd check with other localities.

I was trying to decide if I should go ahead and drive the old lady to the emergency room to make sure she wasn't dehydrated or that she hadn't sustained some injury when she spoke again. "Who and where are not such important questions. Not what, when or how, either."

"Ma'am?"

"My name and my home obviously mean nothing to me now. But why, why is the question that consumes me."

Why was a question I knew well. Why did my dad have to get sick? Why did he have to hurt so much? Why did he have to die? I quit asking my mom when I understood my questions made her cry. But *why* kept whispering in my heart. "I reckon some questions can never be answered."

"Ridiculous," she said, the worry in her face clearing. "I once made my living answering questions."

I sat straighter. Maybe she was on the verge of remembering. "What exactly did you do?"

Too late. That mask of anxiety already had returned. "Or maybe I was the one posing the questions."

Technology, when it is not being used to mar my credit, is a wonderful thing. The dispatcher called to say that she thought I had in my possession Beatrice Russell, reported missing from a long-term care facility in a city a good two-hour drive away.

"Of course," Mrs. Russell said, her face smoothing out again. "I'm a retired philosophy professor."

"But how in the world could you have gotten here on foot?"

"I took the bus part of the way," she said, opening her purse and withdrawing the snack cake. "I was confused enough to think I needed to visit my parents, but still alert enough to make my way to the station and buy a ticket." She nibbled a little on the cake, then returned it to her purse. "But when I reached my destination, I got turned around, and then I was walking and walking. I'm so glad that gentleman talked me out of taking the shortcut."

"What gentleman?"

"An older gentleman, very nice looking, some sort of European car," she said. "He advised me to stay right where I was, and that he was sending help. Odd, now that I think of it, that he didn't offer me a ride himself, but here you are."

"Did he have long white hair?"

"Who?

"The older gentleman."

"What older gentleman?"

"The older gentleman that advised you help was on

the way."

"Where?" The cloud had descended again.

"It's not important," I said, shifting the transmission into drive and moving forward to turn around and rescue my Stetson. When I reached the spot where my hat sat stuck, I pulled over, leaving the car running so Mrs. Russell could stay cool. "Won't be a minute," I said.

The baton was a lost cause that would have to come out of my next paycheck, but there was no way I was going to leave my hat as a tribute to my humiliation. It was just barely out of my reach, and I'd decided all I had to do was jump and grab. After all, I'd played basketball in high school. I jumped, slipped and landed on my backside in a mudhole, suddenly comprehending why I'd spent my high school career on the bench.

I looked up to see Mrs. Russell advancing toward me with the knitting needle in her hand. There was no evidence of the philosophy professor in her face, just that cloud of confused worry. No doubt she thought she was fending off some lunatic. Wondering whether she'd go for my chest or an eyeball, I scrambled to my feet, hoping I could disarm the professor without hurting her.

She held her weapon out to me. "Here, Cabbie," she said. "Effort is nothing more, and also nothing less, than tension between means and ends in action." When I just stood there, she waved the needle in the direction of my hat.

Then I understood. I took the offering and faced the embankment again, reaching high and jabbing the needle beneath the brim of my Stetson. A quick jerk and the hat somersaulted off the bank and into my hands.

"Thank you, ma'am," I said, giving the needle back to her. Maybe I should have kept it, but she'd already had enough taken from her.

"I'd like to go home now," Mrs. Russell said,

depositing the needle back in her massive purse.

"Yes, Ma'am," I said, and helped her back to the car. Maybe I could sweet talk the dispatcher into persuading the chief that returning Mrs. Russell safely to the facility qualified as protecting and serving. And maybe on the return trip I could hunt for jaguar.

"You are the most helpful cabbie I've ever met," she said. "Always remember your humanity, and forget the rest, and you'll do fine." She squeezed my arm. "Promise me you'll remember."

"I'll remember," I said, tucking her into the passenger seat. "I promise."

Epilogue
Twilight Dawn

The State Fair of West Virginia is my favorite manifestation of heaven. Right now, I'm sitting on the tailgate of Major Goshen's dark green Chevrolet pickup, in the field where the fairgoers park. Maj. Goshen unpacks a picnic lunch.

"I believe this truck is a little before your time," I say. In the distance, I can see the gigantic double Ferris wheel and I hear the happy shrieks of children enjoying ride after ride. Heaven is ticket free.

"Best-looking truck ever made." Maj. Goshen smiles, and in the flash of those dimples I can see where young Paul gets some of his rascal's ways. "1957, just like my dad's."

1957. Back on earth, a white man and a black woman could not have shared a meal so easily. I still have questions about the way the world turns, but I'm willing to allow there's a larger pattern that I can't see, just like those folks who couldn't imagine how I could design a quilt with mismatched pieces of fabric.

"I figured you being more partial to red, like your boy."

Maj. Goshen hands me a cheese sandwich on soft white bread. "Green was my dad's favorite color. He said it was the color of growing things."

I don't know if my father had a favorite color. Or a favorite baseball team. Or whether he lived to see Jackie Robinson earn Rookie of the Year. Or whether he had a favorite song. Or if he ever thought of the baby that he left to someone else's care.

The major reaches for a gallon jar of tea that I know will be good and sweet. "You still keeping a close eye on Hope County?"

"That boy of yours has a good heart," I answer. "He has the makings of a fine man."

"He'll find his own way."

"I reckon we all do." I take a bite of sandwich, then wash it down with tea served in a glass the major won at the dime toss. Whole grains and sugar-free products have no place in heaven. Heaven is soft and sweet.

I'm enjoying another swig of tea when I see a man walking toward us. He's wearing worn work clothes and his body looks just as worn, stooped with burden like he's spent years in a coal mine. I've never seen a picture of my papa, but I know it's him.

He's standing in front of us, not saying a word, tears running down a face much darker than mine. I want to ask him the question that burned inside me for ten decades: Did you really have to give me up? Did you really have to go away? But my trembling mouth can't talk.

Then he opens his arms and says, "Can you give your papa a hug?" I just sit there. How can I give love to someone I don't even know?

Maj. Goshen slips a hand under my elbow to help me down from the tailgate. "Go on," he says. "It's time." Suddenly, the cross-examination I'd rehearsed over and over no longer matters. What answer could satisfy me, anyway? I run to my father, the years falling away from me. By the time I reach his open arms, I'm a little girl just happy to see her papa.

He sweeps me into his arms, and I smell the tobacco and sweat of a man who's worked hard all his life. Then I feel him straighten as sorrow starts to slip from his shoulders. "My sweet child." In that one sentence of mingled grief and joy, I hear everything I need.

Notes

Story Assistance
Arlene Anderson, Dwayne Anderson, Michael Brumfield, Vicki Dean, Robert Everhart, David Jackson, Ed Martin, Phyllis Wilson Moore and Lesley Toliver.

First Readers
Ruth Anderson, Pat Baker, Gina Vitolo and Julie Weston.

Technical Assistance: Layton Gillen, Brooke Gillen

"Bark Like You Mean Business"
The Edith Wharton quotes are from *Ethan Frome.*

"Mr. Kotes"
Quotations source: Bartleby.com.

"Driver's Ed"
Seth's meditation is from Thich Nhat Hanh. This and other mindfulness verses, from *Present Moment Wonderful Moment: Mindfulness Verses for Daily Living,* published by Parallax Press, can be read at www.belicfnet.com/story/30/story_3087_1.html

"Appraisal"
The story of the pioneer woman is based upon a historical incident related by author June Langford Berkley.

"Remember Your Humanity"
"Effort is nothing more . . ." is cited from John Dewey. "The Psychology of Effort," *Philosophical Review 6,* (1897): 43-56. www.brocku.ca/MeadProject/Dewey/Dewey_1897.html

"Remember your humanity, and forget the rest," is quoted from "The Peril of Universal Death," written by Bertrand Russell and Albert Einstein in 1955. The entire text of this peace manifesto is available at http://www.pugwash.org/about/manifesto.htm

Acknowledgments

In my bookcase sits a hardcover volume given to me nearly four decades ago. It has followed me through all my moves, this children's book I received as a birthday present.

The cover features four sisters sitting in a parlor. The book, a Golden Press edition of Louisa May Alcott's *Little Women*, was a gift from my own sister, Patricia Jackson. I didn't consciously decide that I, too, would become a writer just like the character Jo, but I believe that gift planted a seed.

I cherish the book even more now, because it is a tangible reminder of my sister, whose battle with cancer ended Jan. 17 of this year.

A big sister is irreplaceable. She's a mentor, a role model, a friend and sometimes a cheerleader. She's the one who goes to the trouble of making homemade cranberry sauce and stuffing for the Thanksgiving turkey. She's the one with the patience to spend day after day making overtures to an abandoned dog so abused that it cringes from human contact. She's the one who makes the extra effort to drive to a certain post office just so her family and friends can receive Christmas cards stamped with a Santa Claus, Ind., cancellation mark.

One day when I thought I could not bear the pain of Patricia's absence, I picked up *Little Women* and found the chapter where Jo must face the death of her sweet sister Beth. Sitting at her sister's bedside, Jo says, "I used to think I couldn't let you go. But I'm learning to feel that I don't lose you, that you'll be more to me than ever and death can't part us, though it seems to." I found comfort in reading Beth's gentle response " ... love is the only thing that we can carry with us when we go, and it makes the end so easy."

Patricia carried a lot of love with her.

She always loved to read, too. She belonged to the Marylee Vogel Book Club, a peppy group that often takes field trips to parallel the books the members read. When my second book, *The Bingo Cheaters*, was published, Patricia and her library's branch manager, the fantastic Gail Russell, spearheaded a reading that turned into a rollicking production of the title story. Patricia, her fellow club members, and even our mother assumed the roles of the story's characters. Patricia somehow came up with a recipe to approximate the Lucious Lime Salad mentioned in the story, one small bit of evidence of her creative, generous and meticulous nature.

After Patricia's memorial service, those same book club members served the family dinner — at the library. She would have loved that.

Gail, who also is a minister, presided over Patricia's service, sharing warm memories and issuing a message of encouragement to each family member. To me, she said that Patricia would have wanted me to keep writing. In her honor, I hope to do just that.

I want to encourage you to write, too. For Patricia's last birthday, I wrote her a letter, telling her how much I loved her, and how much I appreciated her for everything she'd done and for simply being who she was.

There's someone in your life who needs that letter from you. Please write it and send it today.